CHRISTMAS EVE AT PICCADILLY CIRCUS
BY
KELLY MATTHEWS

Christmas Eve at Piccadilly Circus

Chapter One

There were days when Darcy wished she hadn't inherited her grandmother's pub, and today, as she ran up the steps of Bond Street tube station, she wished she hadn't come to London at all. A downpour of rain greeted her as she reached the busy pavement, soaking her to the skin.

'Oh, thank you *very* much!' she grumbled, cursing the rain that only added to her ever-increasing despair. She pulled up the collars of her biker jacket, tucked in her scarf and walked down Davies' Street, turning onto Oxford Street. Standing on the curb, waiting for the passing traffic to stop, she glanced up at the Christmas decorations strung across the buildings, batted the rain out of her lashes and saw that Christmas had arrived in London. But not even cheery old Santa Claus swinging precariously from the wire could offer her respite from the worry that plagued her today. When she made it to Old Bond Street, she took shelter under the awning of the *Chanel* store, soaked through to her skin. As if she didn't have enough to contend with today, her friend Trudy had rung her early to ask if she'd meet her at a dress shop. It wasn't where Darcy wanted to be the first thing on a Saturday morning, but she figured she had to be there to support her friend. They had known each other since they were both at nursery school in Wales. Trudy shared her packed lunch with Darcy and from that moment on they were inseparable until Trudy went to university in London.

Time was getting on and the rain kept pouring. Darcy knew it wouldn't stop soon and decided to make a move, but as she was leaving, a black Mercedes with blacked-out windows pulled up on the roadside that piqued her interest. As a self-confessed nosey parker, Darcy watched as the driver dressed in a dark suit get out and opened the passenger door. The one thing that excited her the most about walking around London was the celebrities she'd spot. Only last week she met Boy George, one of her favourite singers. She pulled out her phone from inside her pocket and was about to snap a picture, when she saw a walking stick touch the pavement and a small old lady in a green coat heaving herself out of the car. At first, she thought it may be Angela Lansbury, but the woman's thick Scottish accent soon ruled that out. Disappointed she didn't recognise her, she smiled at the woman entering the store and thought she'd better leave because the window dresser was looking at her suspiciously. She stepped out of the shelter, wincing as icy raindrops ran down her neck to her bra. Shivering and feeling underdressed for such a posh shop she tried to assemble her now soaked hair into a neat bun. She ran the rest of the way and arrived outside the entrance to the shop. Trudy was waving her inside, and Darcy pushed the door open, aware that her shoes were squelching and squeaking as she entered.

She noticed there were a few side glances her way from the shop assistants, but she smiled at them and went to join Trudy standing beside a rail of white designer gowns. One of which she imagined cost more than she had spent on clothes in her entire lifetime.

'So, I just about made it,' she shrugged off her sopping wet jacket.

Trudy arched an eyebrow and looked at her from head to toe. 'Haven't you heard of umbrellas? Or buses? Or taxis, even?'

Darcy threw her jacket towards a white-backed chair with velvet lining and heard Trudy gasp with horror. Realising her mistake, she picked it up and put it down on the floor before taking her seat, except she knew that her wet hair was dripping onto the plush lining.

'It wasn't raining when I left. Anyway, I've got a lot on my mind right now.'

'Like what?' Trudy asked, concern in her voice.

'Oh, let's forget it for today.'

'No, no. Tell me what's wrong.'

'The pub is in trouble. Nan left behind a huge debt, unfortunately.'

'I didn't know. Why don't you tell me these things?' She shook her head. 'Here,' she stooped down to her bag and handed her a box of chocolates. 'I brought us a treat while we shop and please use the wipes for your hands before touching anything.'

'You know me well.' She opened the box and Trudy reached over, snatched a few and popped them in her mouth.

'If you eat anymore, you'll have to get your wedding dress adjusted,' Darcy joked, biting into the soft caramel centred chocolate with no regrets. She gave Trudy a smug look and popped another into her mouth, oblivious to the drips of rain rolling down her cheeks.

'He's marrying me for my inner beauty...'

'If you say so,' Darcy remarked, watching her pluck a hideous dress off the metal rack.

'Now tell me what you think about this one?'

Darcy shot back in her chair, grossed-out by the peach, frilly number she thrust in front of her face.

'If you fancy yourself as Peaches and Cream Barbie, then knock yourself out.'

Trudy's face lit up. 'Really? Do you mean...'

'No,' she scoffed; mortified she'd even consider the monstrosity. 'You're not buying it, so pick something else. Please. I can't be seen with you wearing that, no way.'

'But I loved Peaches and Cream Barbie,' she mockingly pouted. 'Oh alright, be honest why don't you? No, you're right. I'll look a right bloody frump, won't I?'

They both laughed and Trudy went back to the large rack of dresses. 'So, what are you going to do about the pub? Sell it and make a tidy profit?' she asked, lifting up dress after dress.

Darcy shook her head and shrugged. 'No idea. I'm having to rent out the upstairs flat to make ends meet. I've got a guy coming tomorrow to look at it. He's a university professor, so I'm guessing he's a boring old git that won't give me too much grief.'

'I hope he's rich and handsome for your sake.' Trudy blurted it out so loud that one of the shop assistants giggled.

Darcy wished the ground would swallow her friend up, spitting her out on the other side of the door. Even though she was grateful she offered to buy the bridesmaid dresses, Darcy still felt uncomfortable. There was no way she'd be able to afford to shop on Bond Street otherwise, more like TK Maxx if she was feeling plush.

'As long as he pays his rent on time I don't care. So, have you picked the bridesmaid dresses yet?' she asked when her phone rang. She fished around her bag for her phone and checked the caller ID. 'It's work. I need to take this.' She pressed the accept button and the moment she did she heard her barmaid, Jess, begging her to come back to the pub to sort out a stroppy customer. 'I won't be long. Just offer him a packet of crisps or something in the meantime. Maybe that will pacify him until I get there.' She looked up at Trudy and said she had to leave.

'You're hoping a packet of crisps will help resolve a pub brawl?' she laughed. 'Before you go,' Trudy went through her handbag. 'Take this Oyster card and get the frickin' bus or you'll end up ill. Oh, and wait. You can take the rest of the chocolates, too. I'd better watch my waistline.'

'Thanks,' said Darcy, trying not to laugh as she took the box and shoved it into her handbag.

Chapter Two

Back in Paddington, Darcy pounded up Praed Street, wondering what would greet her when she walked into the pub. She had only owned it for the last couple of months and she wasn't sure if she wanted to sell it on or make a go of the business. Having packed up her life in Swansea, a city by the sea, and moving to a hectic London, she found it was taking a lot more adjustment than she originally thought.

The Churchill was situated on a corner, next to a newsagent and a takeaway on the side street. Its gold letterings above the green-painted framework was in desperate need of a fresh coat and needed an extra *L*. Several of the windows were cracked and needed replacing – but that would involve money and that was something she just didn't have. As she approached, a short, slim man wearing a brown suit stepped out of the pub and waved to her. It was Mr. Jones. A few of the locals had told her he was a permanent fixture of *The Churchill*, a part of the furniture, even. And as she found out, he was very knowledgeable about the pub's history and the local area. He became her support when she opened the doors for the first time, so she didn't mind letting him in early as she wasn't sure if he had anywhere to go.

She waited for the on-coming taxi to pass and crossed the road, now carrying the sodden chocolate box. She had just made it to the opposite side of the road when she felt the box break from underneath and the contents fell by her feet.

'Not having a good day, are you?' Mr. Jones exclaimed in his Cockney accent.

Darcy threw the empty, mangled box on the floor and took a deep breath.

'No, I'm not, Mr. Jones.' She dropped to her haunches to pick up the chocolates now covered with cigarette ash and slung them back into the mangled box. Mr. Jones swooped in to help her.

'Left the coffee ones, eh?' he asked, blowing the ash off and inspecting it.

Darcy looked at him incredulously. 'You're not going to eat that, surely?' she asked, screwing up her face in disgust.

'We used to eat anything in my day it's how we built up our immune systems.' He popped it in his mouth. 'It's no wonder kids these days are catching everything under the sun.'

She shook her head in disbelief, stepped around him, and went inside the pub, half expecting to find the place trashed by an angry punter. Her tense shoulders drooped when all she saw were two elderly gents sitting around a table watching the latest news on a television that looked like it stepped out of the eighties. Arthur, one of her regulars raised a hand to say hello and then pointed to the screen.

'They're forecasting a bad winter. My arse. They say that every year.'

'Hello, Arthur,' she said. 'Maybe the news report is as old as the television,' she laughed.

Darcy wondered what the fuss had been about and walked toward the arched-shaped bar where Jess, her part-time barmaid, and fashion student, was standing wiping glasses.

'Where's the drama?'

Jess waved a dismissive hand. 'It was fine. Sorry I had to drag you from your shopping trip. It was lucky your new tenant stepped in to help.'

Surprised to hear this as she wasn't expecting him until tomorrow, Darcy glanced around the room. 'My tenant?' she questioned, confused. 'I don't have one yet.'

'Yes, it's that guy who called you a week ago to arrange a viewing.'

'Yeah, I know that, but he's not coming until tomorrow.'

'Well,' she pointed over Darcy's shoulder. 'He's here.'

Darcy swung around, staring into the ice-blue eyes of a dark-haired stranger smiling down at her.

'It's Darcy Tanner, isn't it? We spoke on the phone last week.' He proffered his hand.

'Yes. Sorry, I wasn't expecting you until tomorrow.' She shook it. He had a firm grip and looked absolutely stunning. Definitely not the old git she had imagined.

'My flight was early, so I'd thought I'd take a chance. If it's not convenient, I can come back later.'

'Oh, no, no that's okay.' She panicked. 'Would you excuse me for one moment? I need to get the key.' She turned to Jess serving behind the bar. 'Give Mr. Hanlon whatever drink he wants - on the house.'

She hurried to the other side of the bar where Mr. Jones was sipping his pint.

'Why the ants in your pants?' he asked, holding his glass mid-way to his mouth.

Darcy called over Jess.

'I can't show him the flat because I haven't even finished the decorating upstairs. I meant to do it this evening,' she whispered.

Darcy noticed Jess went quiet and raised a brow at Mr. Jones as though they knew something she didn't. She followed her gaze and gave him a questioning look.

'What have you done?'

'Don't worry, take him upstairs. It's all been sorted for you.'

'It was a tip when I left it this morning. Hang on, what do you mean it has been sorted?'

'Trust me. Take him up and show him around the place. It'll be fine.'

'Why?' she insisted. 'What have you done?'

'I overheard you talking about it, and so I asked Jess to let me and Harry up there. We cleaned it up for you. No charge.'

'You did?' she asked, surprised.

Mr. Jones nodded. 'Alright, I'll accept two free pints for the service.'

Relieved, Darcy didn't know what else to say and thanked him. She called over Mr. Hanlon.

'It's Gareth, please.' He rose to his feet and strode over to the bar.

'Sorry about that. I'll show you the flat now.'

They exited through the main door of the pub, turned the corner and walked along the pavement to the lane at the back of the building. Darcy pushed open the back door and walked up the garden path. She pointed to a metal staircase leading the way to flat's front door.

'I know it's a pain to get to, so may I suggest that you don't walk up here drunk,' she laughed, looking for the correct key on the chain. 'Although, there's an entrance through my flat you could use but it's locked, so you don't have to worry about creepy landlords sneaking up on you.' She stopped, realising what she had said. 'I didn't mean that the way it came out.'

Gareth laughed. 'I get what you're saying,' he said, 'Hey, I just thought of something. If I want a pint, do I ring the bell and you'll deliver it?' he said jokingly. 'Or could I just use your door?'

Darcy chuckled. 'Delivery is extra on top of the rent.'

When she arrived in London, she intended to live in the flat above the pub herself, but the financial constraints meant it was wiser if she rented it out until she got the business back on its feet.

She unlocked the door and pushed it open, hoping Mr. Jones had cleaned it like he said he did. The amount of free drinks she had given him over the last month when he had been short of money, she thought it was a nice gesture of him to help. Besides, as she found out, he liked to feel useful and would often offer to collect the empty glasses.

'I hope you'll feel at home...' Darcy froze by the door unsure whether she should allow him to enter. She flicked on the light switch to make sure her eyes weren't deceiving her and stepped inside the flat. She swallowed hard, looking at the walls that were once a beautiful magnolia. 'It's like a seventies revival. What the bloody hell has he done?' she shrieked, trying to take it all in.

Gareth snorted with laughter.

Mortified, Darcy walked around the living room, staring at the multi-coloured floral explosion that was beaming back at her. She turned to Gareth, who was now in hysterics. 'I don't know what to say. It wasn't like this when I left the pub this morning, I promise.'

'It's okay, honey. I saw the before pictures on the internet and I know that it wasn't like this. Bloody hell, it reminds me of those viewfinder things we had when we were kids,' he laughed and took out his phone to snap a picture.

Darcy realised what had happened and felt her blood boil. 'I can't believe that idiot. I found that wallpaper in the cupboard last week. I meant to take it to the charity shop but obviously forgot and left it lying around,' she exhaled and shook her head at his handy work.

'Don't worry about it; it's an easy fix.' Gareth put a friendly hand on her shoulder to reassure her that he was alright with it and laughed again. 'It's not like I'm going to be here permanently, is it? Look, where do I sign?' He touched her shoulder again trying to regain his composure, except he couldn't and laughed even harder.

Darcy finally saw the funny side too and laughed.

'What's going on up here?' Called Jess from the bottom of the stairs.

'See, there's the spare door.' She went to open it. 'Jess, come up here and fetch my phone and that twit with you,' she shouted.

'By "that twit" I take it you mean Mr. Jones?'

'Who else?'

There was the sounds of feet clomping up the stairs. Jess poked her head around the door and her mouth fell open with shock.

'What is this?'

'Ask him,' Darcy pointed at Mr. Jones, surveying his work with pride.

'What's wrong with it? You left the rolls on the table. I assumed that's what you wanted putting up.'

Gareth stepped forward. 'It's fine. I'm still taking the place. But if you want it repainted, I don't mind doing it one weekend.'

'You're too kind,' Darcy said, catching Jess winking at her. She glared at her back.

'I think I will love living here. Is it okay if I bring my stuff around tomorrow? I'm staying at a hotel tonight just across the road.'

'Sure. I'll get your key before you go.' She turned to head down the stairs Jess had used. 'We may as well use this now. But I'll lock it for you.'

'Don't mind me, it's convenient anyway.'

'Why don't you stay for a drink or two if you're not in a hurry to go anywhere?'

'I'd love to, but I have a meeting at the college. Maybe another time?' he took the key she handed him and put it in his pocket.

'Great, I'll walk you to the door,' said Darcy.

Darcy stood behind the bar strumming her fingers as she watched the only two punters she had walk out.

'Goodnight, love,' they said as they drunkenly exited.

She checked the clock hanging above the bar. 'It's only nine. Even my local back home was jumping at nine, and there were only thirty-odd people in the village.'

'Including the sheep?' Mr. Jones asked.

'Hey, no sheep jokes, its racist,' she laughed. 'But, yeah, including the sheep.'

'I don't think the sheep will mind.' Mr. Jones slid his empty glass across the bar. 'Give me a coffee, Jess.' He then turned back to Darcy. 'When your gran was here, this place used to be packed to the rafters every night. And when your great gran was here. God bless her soul...'

'You knew my great-grandmother? Exactly how old are you, Mr. Jones?' she asked.

'Old enough,' he laughed. 'Your great grandmother, Mary, pulled a pint for Churchill once in this pub, did you know that?'

Intrigued, Darcy took a seat on a stool next to him. 'No, I didn't. I know little about either of my grandmothers if I'm honest.'

'They were wonderful women, and when they went, they took the heart of this place with them. It's never been the same.'

'I've never seen a picture of my great gran, Lily. Dad said there wasn't any he can recall. I've always wondered what she looked like.'

'You haven't seen a picture of her at all?' he asked, surprised. 'See that,' he pointed to a wooden cupboard under the bar. 'Have you looked in there yet?'

'No. Why?' She looked at the cupboard wondering how she could have missed it.

'Open it.'

Darcy got off the stool and walked around the bar. She twisted the handle and opened the door. Inside was a brown envelope that she pulled out. 'This?'

'Yes, I'm surprised you haven't found it already. Didn't you explore the place when you got here?'

'Barely. I was too focused on opening and making money.' Darcy opened it and tipped the contents out onto the bar. There was a pile of postcards bound with a red ribbon. 'What are these?'

'Love letters between your great nan and a guy she met here at *The Churchill*.'

'Why were they kept in the cupboard?' she asked, untying the ribbon.

'Your grandmother, Mary, kept them in there. No idea why to be honest. But everyone who came here knew about the letters.'

'Well, I didn't,' she remarked, but then realised that her father had spent no time in the pub after he'd moved to Wales and met her mother. 'So, what's the story?' she asked, reading the hedgehog scrawl that belonged to a man named Walter.

'Your great gran and Walter were very much in love. I'd say he was her soulmate. Anyway, he went away to war, and they never saw each other again except for one brief meeting when his ship docked. I believe they wrote to each other for two years, and when they were due to meet on Christmas Eve at Piccadilly Circus in 1944, his ship sank in the Atlantic. So tragic. So very tragic.'

'Oh no, that's really sad.' Tears welled in her eyes as she read what she believed to be the last postcard he ever sent. It was dated August 1944.

Dear Lily, my darling,

I was so happy to receive your letter. I am sorry to hear about the bomb, but I am relieved to know that you are okay.

My ship is due back in Blighty this Christmas, and would love to meet you as there's something I really need to ask you. Shall we arrange to meet on Christmas Eve at Piccadilly Circus? I'll be the one standing by the Fountain of Anteros.

All my love,

Walter.

'Wasn't the fountain boarded up during the war?' asked Darcy, proud of herself for knowing this fact.

'Yes, but I believe that's where they would've met if it hadn't been for the tragedy.'

'So where are the pictures of them?' she asked, going through the postcards once more.

'No picture? Well, there should be a picture of both of them in there. I saw it with my own two eyes. It was taken over there,' he pointed to the table by the window. 'If I remember rightly, the window was covered with blackout blinds because of the war, and your great gran and Walter were sitting on that very table having a drink.'

Darcy glanced over her shoulder at the table. 'I wonder what happened to the picture.'

'Me too. It's very strange that it's not in there.'

Darcy went up to the table and gently ran her fingers along the grooves. 'Oh, I've got the chills, Mr. Jones. In a good way, mind you.'

'Yes, those were the days. This place was the local hotspot for soldiers, did you know that?'

'No, I didn't. If the walls could talk, eh?' said Darcy, returning to the bar.

'Yes, if only. I'm sure it would have amazing stories to tell.'

Chapter Three

'Good morning, Mr. Jones.' Darcy arrived at the pub at around eight-thirty with the milk she'd bought from the shop next door. She was cold, hungry, and wanted nothing more than to get inside for her first cup of coffee before she opened for the day.

'I bought you a coffee and a bagel, love.' He held up a polystyrene cup and a paper bag.

Surprised, Darcy thanked him and fumbled in her bag for the keys. 'So, what's the occasion?' she asked, slipping the key into the lock of the black chipped door. 'Is it to apologise for the wallpapering catastrophe? If it is, there's no harm done.'

'Oh, I know that. No, there's no reason. Well, okay. Jess told me you are having trouble with the pub and you're thinking about selling it.' He patted the side of his nose. 'I won't tell a soul; you know, I'm very discreet like that...'

Darcy sighed. 'It's not a secret, but I don't really want to discuss it right now if that's okay with you.' About to step inside, she saw a bundle of assorted envelopes on the welcome mat and bent down to collect them. 'I'll have the coffee in a moment, Mr. Jones. Just put it on the bar.' She went straight to her living quarters which also served as her office at the back of the pub. There was a small passage that separated the very tiny kitchen and living area and there was a door to the left, which was her bedroom. She pushed open the living room door and threw the mail onto her floral sofa. It hadn't been decorated for over twenty years, and it still boasted a 1930s fire surround.

'Still haven't decorated for Christmas, I see?' Mr. Jones asked.

Darcy went back out into the bar and rolled her eyes. 'No, Mr. Jones, I haven't had the time. Besides, it's only the middle of November.'

She spotted the cardboard box of decorations on the windowsill she had found in the cupboard. She didn't want to think about Christmas at the moment. Although she was looking forward to it as she did every year, this year it felt different, as if something was missing. She thought back to last Christmas when she returned home from work to find her fiancé cheating on her in their bed. Anger coursed through her body once more, but then she talked herself out of the feeling. She had a lot going for her at the moment, even if it didn't really seem like it right now.

She put her bag on the chair, remembering how Scott, her ex-boyfriend had giving it to her last Christmas. In a fit of rage, she emptied the contents onto the coffee table and held out the bag to Mr. Jones who had just walked into the room.

'The next person to walk into the pub, give this to them' She dangled the bag as though it was poison.

'Are you serious? Isn't that the posh designer handbag worth two hundred pounds you were bragging about the first day you came?'

'Hardly call it bragging, but yeah, it is.'

He looked at her incredulously. 'Give it away?' he asked again and took it from her.

'Yes, give it away.' She flicked her hand.

'If that's what you want.'

There was a knock on the door. Darcy was busy cleaning the mascara from her cheeks.

'I'll get it.' Mr. Jones walked out of the living room to answer it while Darcy got up from the sofa, deciding she needed to check on the stock. She went out the back garden and down the cellar. Christmas was coming, and she needed to boost business. If she couldn't make the pub work, she would have to sell the pub and find somewhere else to live. It wasn't what she wanted. She rolled a barrel and connected it to the mains when she thought she heard someone call her.

'Darcy,' Mr. Jones called her back into the pub.

'What is it?' she asked, irritated. She opened the door and saw Mr. Jones sitting in his chair looking pleased. 'I got rid of your bag for you.'

'You did?'

'Don't look so shocked. Now you can get on with the rest of your life.'

She slapped her hand across her forehead and went back into her living room without saying a word. How could she tell him that she was only joking with him? She flounced onto the sofa and sobbed.

'Yoo-hoo, it's only me,' Trudy hailed from the pub.

Darcy snatched the box of tissues on the sideboard, plucked one out and wiped her eyes.

'Hi, Trude, I wasn't expecting you today,' she said, acting as if nothing had happened.

'I'm not putting up with this.' Trudy walked in, threw her handbag on the chair, and sat next to Darcy. 'If the pub is giving you grief, sell it on, love. Nobody will hate you for it.'

'It's not the pub for once.' She sniffed back tears.

'What then?'

Darcy exhaled. 'I was just angry over what happened last Christmas and gave my bag to Mr. Jones to get rid of, which he did. Now it's gone.'

'So, you're crying over the bag or that bastard who cheated on you?' She wrapped an arm around Darcy's shoulders.

'Both, I suppose.' She blew her nose into a tissue.

'Why are you wasting good tears over a jerk like him?'

'I was with him for a year and a half, Trude.'

'And how many times out of that was he away working? I say at least seven months out of the year.'

'What are you saying?'

'What I'm saying is, did you love him or are you missing what could've been?'

Trudy wasn't the kind of person to mince her words, but Darcy agreed. '

'I suppose in some way, you're right. I hardly saw him even when he was home. His job would take him all over the world. It was like having a relationship with my phone because that's the only way we communicated.'

'Good, now you're seeing sense. But there's one other thing. Remember that business lunch my Harvey put on? Well, he and Scott got talking, and Harvey, the idiot what he is, gave him a job. Here, in London.'

'You're joking?' Darcy looked at Trudy, shocked. She didn't want to see him.

'No. I didn't want to tell you before you came here, otherwise, you wouldn't have come, and you would never have known you could run a pub. I'm sorry, Darcy, but with the size of London, I doubt you'd ever bump into him.'

Darcy rubbed her temples which were throbbing with all the stress. She came to London to de-stress, and yet she was under more stress than she had been before she moved.

'Okay,' she took a deep breath. 'That part of my life is now over, and yes, London is a big place and yes, I've got a pub to make a success of.' She turned to look at Trudy. 'I can do this, can't I?'

'Of course you bloody well can. Look, I'm sorry, Darce. It was out of my hands. You know I would never have agreed to it if I knew what he was planning.'

'Shit. Well at least London is bigger than Swansea, eh? There's fat chance of me bumping into him.' There was still a small chance that she would. She didn't know how she would cope if she saw him. Did she even want to see him again? She really didn't know if she could answer that.

'That's the spirit. Now, do you want a cup of coffee before you open the pub?'

'Yes, please.' She rummaged through the junk from her bag, looking for the postcards. 'Oh no, the postcards, they're gone.'

'What postcards?' Trudy asked from the kitchen.

'My great grandmother's postcards. They were here, in amongst all my stuff. Oh no, I think I put them in the pocket.'

'Why did you give the bag away, anyway? It was expensive.'

'Because I didn't want any reminders of him. But that's another story right now. I need to find these cards.'

'Slow down.' Trudy put a mug of coffee on the table. 'And start from the very beginning.'

Sweeping the pavement outside the pub, Darcy, who was concentrating on the crisp packets that were getting away, flinched when a set of brown loafers appeared in her line of vision.

'Sorry.' She looked up and moved aside for the pedestrian to move.

'No need to clean up, especially for me,' Gareth said, carrying a holdall and two suitcases. 'But I thank you anyway.'

'Hello there. Moving in now, are you?' she asked, straightening herself up.

'Yeah, thank you again for allowing me to stay here for three months. I know you wanted a longer tenant.'

'No bother. It's helping me out...'

Gareth interjected. 'So, I heard you haven't been here long?'

'No. I inherited this place a couple of months ago, and as you can see it needs a lot of work...'

'So that's why you're renting out the flat?'

'No choice. Well, I don't want to hold you up with my troubles.'

'I see that packet is getting away...'

'Bugger.' She went after it and snatched it from the pavement. 'Well, it was no bother. I'm glad you didn't turn around after seeing the wall.' She managed a weak smile.

Gareth's deep blue eyes softened.

'If I can return the favour anytime or if you want a chat, you know where I am. My students say that I'm a good listener.'

'Really? Okay, well, thank you. I'll keep that in mind,' Darcy replied. The offer put a genuine smile on her face. Gareth bid goodbye and headed around the corner to his flat.

Chapter Four

'I hate to point out the obvious, Darcy, but business is slow,' Jess said, sitting behind the bar twirling her blue hair. 'Has sexy from upstairs been down yet?'

Darcy smiled. 'No, he hasn't. Give the man a chance, he only moved in yesterday.' She flipped through the mail. Most were notices for payments, and she shoved them to the side, wanting to forget about them.

'You can't avoid it forever,' Mr. Jones remarked, lifting his pint glass.

'I can for now. It's been a quiet month, and I don't have the money to pay them. Oh, what am I going to do?' She flopped down on the stool, resting her head in her hands. 'We're just not getting the customers thanks to...' She pointed to the window at the pub across the road. 'That big chain.' She couldn't bring herself to say the name.

'It's not just that, love. *The Churchill* has been closed for a long time. Most of the regulars have either moved on or passed on. You need to find a way to re-invent it. Bring it back to life.'

Darcy could see his point and felt her spirits lift a little. 'Yeah, I think you're right, Mr. Jones. Maybe doing a bit of dusting will help me think of that million-dollar idea.'

She set about dusting the shelves when the bell chimed on the door. She spun around, surprised to see Gareth holding her handbag.

'That's a nice bag, Gareth. Do you carry one often?' Jess asked before bursting into laughter.

Darcy wasn't sure what to think. Either he had an exact man bag replica or Mr. Jones had given it to him. Thinking it had to be the latter, she laughed.

'Is that for your makeup?' she questioned with a nod to the bag.

Gareth cleared his throat, his face now red with embarrassment. He looked at Mr. Jones who was smirking behind his pint glass, and then back to Darcy. 'I believe this may be yours?'

Happy to have her bag back, Darcy zoomed in on the bag, hoping the precious postcards were left inside. 'I can't believe it. Did the silly sod give it to you yesterday?' She gave a nod to Mr. Jones who raised an eyebrow at her.

Gareth handed her back the bag. 'I had a feeling it was yours and would've given it back sooner, but I had a meeting and then I totally forgot about it when I saw you yesterday. And no, I didn't take into the meeting,' he laughed, too. 'I left it in my car. Here, I swear I didn't nose in it, but these did fall out of the side pocket.' He reached into his jacket pocket and handed her the postcards.

Darcy's heart leapt for joy. 'Thank you. You have no idea what these mean to me.'

'I think I can guess, actually. They're quite special, it seems.'

Darcy looked up at him expectantly.

'Sorry, I mean, I read them. I hope you don't mind, but they fell out of the bag. Do you have an idea who the couple may be? Because if you don't, I may be able to help with your research.'

'I do actually,' she replied, excited to have the cards back. 'Lily is my great nan. She owned the pub. In fact, you've given me an idea. I don't know anything about Walter, so that could be something to look into.'

'Well if you need any help, you know where to ask. As a history professor, I'll be more than happy to offer my expertise.'

'Thank you. Oh, and you may be wondering why he gave you the bag?' Darcy asked, walking to the bar and picked up a clean glass off the shelf.

'I did wonder, yes.' He sat on the barstool.

'I wanted to get rid of it, but when I asked,' she rolled her eyes at Mr. Jones, 'he took me literally when I said to give it to the first person to walk into the pub.'

Gareth smiled. 'Luckily it was me then. I did wonder what was going on, but I was in such a rush.'

She waved the glass. 'Do you want a drink?' she asked. 'By the way, was there anything else you wanted?'

'No drink for me thanks, maybe this evening. If it's fine with you, I'm going to move the furniture around a bit, so if you hear World War Three upstairs, you know what it is.' He winked.

'No bother, I hope you like it up there.'

'The paper is intense, but other than that, it feels like home already. Well, I'd best be off.'

'Have a good day and thanks again.'

As Gareth was leaving, Trudy walked in carrying the dresses she had bought. She looked up at Gareth and smiled at him as they passed. 'Good afternoon, everyone,' she intoned as she stepped into the pub. 'He's gorgeous, isn't he?' she commented as she put the dresses on an empty table and then pulled off her coat.

Mr. Jones laughed. 'Oh, thank you very much. Much obliged.'

Confusion swept across her face. 'I meant...'

'I know who you meant, you silly bugger,' he chuckled again.

Darcy shrugged. 'I suppose he is.'

'Give over, you know he is.'

'Alright, he is, now let's see what dresses you ended up buying.' Darcy waited with anticipation as she watched Trudy unzip the bags. If her first choice at the store was anything to go by, she didn't have much hope for what she was about to reveal.

'Ta-da!' Trudy pulled out a red sequined dress that was better suited to a drag queen.

'Are you having a laugh right now, because if you are it isn't funny,' Darcy exclaimed, thinking it wasn't the sort of dresses they sold at the shop.

A customer burst out laughing. 'Sorry, but that is just awful. Bloody awful.'

'What's wrong with it?' said Trudy, oblivious to why they were laughing.

Darcy cleared her throat, trying desperately to stop laughing. 'Trudy, we need to talk about elegance and class,' said Darcy, now heading to the bar. 'I'll get us some wine, go and sit down.'

DARCY DUNKED THE MOP into the bucket of filthy water and took a moment to reflect. Apart from the two regulars and Mr. Jones, who was reading the newspaper at the bar, the pub was quiet. Deciding she needed a break, she sat down at the table next to the window and opened her laptop to pay the few bills that she could afford, albeit reluctant to pay.

'Everything alright?' Jess asked joining her at the table.

Darcy leaned back against the seat. 'I think I have enough to get through another two months, and that's it. I need to bring in business or sell up.'

'That's a shame because I really like working here. There's so much history packed in one place...'

Darcy closed her laptop. 'That's it,' she exclaimed, loud enough to get everyone's attention.

'What do you mean, Darcy?'

She couldn't believe she hadn't thought of it before. 'History. That's what's going to make this place alive again.' She slammed her hand down on the table and took a moment to appreciate the vision she could see playing out in her head.

'It is?' Jess asked, confused.

Darcy rose to her feet. 'Look around you. The answer to my problems has been staring me in the face all this time.'

Jess rose an eyebrow, still not understanding what was going on. 'It has?'

Darcy sat back down, too excited to know what to do with herself. 'Finding my grandmother Lily's postcards has given me an insight into her past that I would never have known about if I hadn't come here. Look,' she shifted her chair around to face Jess. 'When I was given this place, I honestly didn't want anything to do with it, I mean, look around you, it's like a time capsule and would cost me thousands to even compete with those across the road.'

'How is this going to save the business though? I'm lost.'

'Me too,' said Mr. Jones, listening from his usual seat by the bar.

'Well, this it. I don't want to be like them. *The Churchill* is unique, so why don't I turn it into a 1940s themed pub.'

There was a moment of stunned silence.

'Well you've got my vote,' said Mr. Jones. 'Have you been in the attic yet?'

'No. Dad said the key was lost many years ago. Why?'

'Lost? No. If he had spent more time here, he'd know. The key has always been kept in the jar on the shelf next to the gin. Because that was Lily's favourite drink or so I was told.' He pointed at the brown bottle above the bar.

'You know an awful lot about this place, Mr. Jones,' Darcy commented, as she got up from her chair and reached for the jar. 'So, what's up there?'

'When your dad's mother took over, she put all her mother's furniture and belongings up in the attic. It's why that place back there looks like a concoction of three different eras. Your grandmother wasn't a good decorator.'

'Really? Why didn't you tell me this before?'

He laughed. 'You never asked. I just assumed you knew everything about your family.'

Darcy tipped the jar, and a small key fell out into the palm of her hand. 'Well, I never! I'd better call my father later and tell him all about this.' As she was about to step down off the chair, Gareth walked in with a bunch of rowdy youngsters that spread out around the bar and took seats at the tables.

'I brought a few of my students along,' he said as he walked up to the bar, smiling in Darcy's direction. 'So how has your day been?' he queried, flipping open his wallet.

Aware her butt was directly in his line of vision, she blushed and got down off the chair. 'It's been interesting. Yours?' she asked, putting the key into the back of her trouser pocket.

'It's been good. I fetched these back as we're going to talk about what we've been learning. I mean, what better way to discuss history than over a pint of beer,' he laughed. The students sat around one of the larger tables, laughing and joking with each other.

'Absolutely,' smiled Darcy, knowing she had made the right choice about keeping the pub. 'Actually, now you mention history, I want to thank you for returning the cards,' she poured the beer. 'They were written by my great gran and her lover during World War Two, but you probably know that anyway,' she laughed.

'Curiosity got the best of me, I'm afraid,' he replied. 'What a find though. Do you know if they ever got married, or...?'

'No, the poor sod drowned before they could meet on Christmas Eve.'

'It's really sad. Maybe you could display the cards in the pub or something as a memorial. It's a shame to keep them hidden in a drawer.'

She put the pitcher of beer on the bar. 'Yeah, I think that's a good idea, actually. Thanks.'

Gareth smiled and handed her a ten-pound note. 'You're welcome. And if you're interested in knowing more about the Blitz, you can come and join us.' He gestured her to the table.

'Thanks, I may just do that.'

Chapter Five

Exhausted after a long day, Darcy said goodbye to Jess and Mr. Jones and then retreated to her living quarters. She flounced down on her grandmother's chair, kicked off her shoes and flicked on the television, but she soon found herself falling asleep. It was early morning when she woke, shivering. She grabbed her cardigan draped over the back of the sofa and went to check the radiator under the window. It was freezing. 'Oh no, please don't be broke,' she grumbled and went into her kitchen to put the kettle on to boil. Her mobile rang, and she pulled it out of her pocket. 'Trudy, what's wrong?' she asked, concerned as it was only just gone half past six.

'I got a message from the Golf club last night. They've double booked our reception and have to give us the deposit back. Darcy, I'm getting married Christmas Eve and I don't have time to find anywhere else.'

'Okay, first thing's first – take a breather, will you? We'll figure this out.' She put the phone on the counter and switched on the speaker while she finished making her tea.

'Did I wake you up?' she asked, sounding wide-awake for such a ghastly hour.

Darcy smiled, pouring milk into her mug and then stirring the tea. 'No, I was awake anyway. The stupid radiator isn't working – probably needs draining or something.'

'Sorry, I forgot you have your own problems. Hey, wait a minute, I may have a solution for both of us.'

'What?' asked Darcy. Intrigued, she leaned against the counter and sipped her tea. It burned her tongue a little.

'Why don't I pay you to host the reception at the pub?'

Darcy spat out her tea.

'I appreciate the thought, but isn't Harvey a millionaire or something? Surely, he wouldn't want his wedding reception in my pub. I don't think it'll be good enough for him and his wealthy guests.'

'Listen to me. I'll pay you the entire deposit. It should cover a few repairs and the cost of food and entertainment. Harvey will have to accept my decision as after all, he said to do what makes me happy, and I'm happy.'

'Wow, so you really do mean this?'

'Yes, it's a perfect solution, don't you agree? I'll meet you later on this afternoon to discuss everything, okay? I've got to go now the cat wants its breakfast.'

Before she opened the pub for the day, Darcy needed to head out to the supermarket for some essentials. She had just closed the door when she saw Gareth walking up the side street. At that moment Darcy couldn't deny that he was handsome and stood on the curb with her breath caught in her throat.

'Morning,' he said, smiling as puffs of smoke escaped his lips. His hands were dug into his coat pockets, and his backpack was slung over his shoulder. 'Cold, isn't it?' he said, stopping to talk.

'Very. Are you off to work?'

'I am.' He gestured her to walk with him. 'Going far?'

'I'm only going to the shop for a few things. Oh, before I forget to ask, is your heating working?'

'Yeah, it's fine. Good of you to ask, not all landlords are that thoughtful,' he laughed. 'Why is there a problem?'

'No, no problem, just checking, you know. Being a good landlady.' She smiled tightly and cleared her throat. 'I meant to ask, what particular period of history do you teach?'

'Most, but I specialise in the first and second world wars. I think it's funny in a way...'

Darcy knew where he was going with this. 'How so?'

'I was thinking about the postcards you found. Have you thought about researching the couple and the pub's history? I'm only asking because if you want to know more, I'd like to lend a helping hand. And some skills.'

'Would you? That's nice of you, thank you. I have thought about it, and I think I'd like to know more. I also have plans to turn the pub into a 1940s themed bar. Do you like the sound of that? Or do you think it's a stupid idea?' She had been thinking about whether or not it would work. It was a big risk, but she couldn't do any worse than she was already doing.

'No, it's not stupid at all. I think it's a great idea. For a start, it's different and not something that's been done before to my knowledge. You have something good going here.' He became distracted by the traffic on the road. 'I need to catch this bus, Darcy. Maybe we can talk later?' he asked, walking backwards.

'Of course. Pop down the bar when you have time.' She waved him off as he stepped onto the bus.

'I may use the secret entrance,' he winked and gave her a wave.

MR. JONES WAS WAITING outside the pub with another old man chatting away when she arrived back with a few carrier bags of shopping.

'Do I see a happier, Darcy today?' he enquired, a small smile tugging at the sides of his mouth.

As she put the key in the lock, she smiled. 'You do, Mr. Jones; that you do. I'll tell you all about in a while. Let me put the shopping away first.'

When she walked past the bar, she saw the pile of postcards next to the pump. 'Oh jeez, I didn't put them away last night.' She picked them up and thought for a moment. She didn't have them at the pub last night with her. Thinking back, she was sure she put them in the living room. 'Strange,' she whispered.

'What's that?' asked Mr. Jones.

'These postcards. I was just talking to Gareth about them, and here they are, like magic.'

'Gareth, eh? That's the lad upstairs, isn't it?'

She put the postcards in her handbag under the bar for safe keeping. 'Yeah, that's him. Nice guy.' She poured a drink for Mr. Jones.

'Oh aye. So, he's nice. Anything else?'

She passed him the drink, noticing an anchor tattooed on his finger. She had never noticed it until now, it was grey and faded but still visible. 'Don't be so cheeky now.' She found him amusing. 'What's that you've got tattooed there?'

Before he could answer, Jess walked into the pub. 'Good morning, everyone,' she sang in a sing-song voice.

'You seem perky today?' Darcy commented.

'I am. Last night you gave me the perfect idea for my end of term fashion project – I'm creating a 1940's themed collection for the modern woman and man. Isn't that exciting?'

'That's fantastic. Why don't you have the show held here?' she suggested, thinking how Trudy wanted the wedding here.

'Really? I'd love that, Darcy, thanks.'

'Well, I have good news. Thanks to Trudy's posh golf club cancelling on her, she's asked me to hold her wedding reception here. But that's not all. She is helping me out with repairs, so I have a lot of work to do and things to organise to get this place back to its former glory.'

Mr. Jones clapped. 'See, things always work out. Well done, love.'

'But I will need help.' She looked at them both with pleading eyes.

'We'll help,' they both replied in unison.

With renewed enthusiasm for the place, Darcy thought about giving the windows a wash and went to the kitchen to fill a bucket of water.

'Jess, do you think you can look after the bar for a little while?' she asked, struggling to carry the heavy bucket across the pub floor to the door, the soapy water splashed about, nearing the edge of the bucket threatening to spill. 'It's not like it's heaving with customers, I know.'

'Of course. Are sure you don't want me to do that?' Jess called out.

'No, it's quite alright,' she said and stepped on the chair she had already brought out. She took the sponge and wiped years' worth of grime off the glass. In gold letterings, *The Churchill* was spelled out across the glass and Darcy wondered why her gran had called it that. She figured she had a lot more to find out about her family and the pub's connection.

'You should get someone to do that for you,' said Trudy, giving her a fright. She held on to the window ledge and gave Trudy a glare.

'Why? It'll be more expensive. It's cheaper if I do it myself.'

'Well give yourself and break and come inside so we can talk.'

Darcy threw the sopping wet sponge into the bucket and got down from the chair, and as she did so, a young couple walking by stopped to look inside the door.

'We're open if you want to come in,' Darcy said.

'Are you?' replied the man. 'I can't remember this place ever being open.' He turned to his partner. 'Fancy a drink?'

His partner nodded, and they entered.

'Maybe I should stand out here washing windows every day to get business, huh?' she said to Trudy.

'Or employ Mr. Jones. He's here often enough,' she laughed.

Darcy emptied the bucket on the roadside into a drain, and walked back into the pub, asking Jess to fetch them over a glass of wine each. She sat down opposite Trudy, who removed her scarf and gloves, setting them aside from her chunky notebook.

Darcy gulped. 'They are all your notes for the wedding?' she asked, already daunted by the task she had yet to give her.

'Just a few things.' She concentrated on flipping through the book. 'Ah. Here we go.' She ripped out the page and handed it to Darcy. 'I managed to cut over a hundred people off the guest list, simply because I'm not people pleasing. So, we should just about fit everyone in here. I've arranged for the flowers and decorations to be delivered a few days before...'

'Okay, so you want me to prepare the finger food?' She looked up expectantly, hoping she didn't want a four-course meal.

'Yes, simple finger food. Nothing too daunting, I promise. And here's the money.' She handed her a cheque.

'*Four thousand*? Where do you want me to get the food from? Harrods?'

Trudy laughed. 'No, but as long as it's good stuff, I don't mind where you go. I want you to use some of that to replace the window and get the signage fixed. I really do think it needs that extra "*L*", don't you?'

Stunned, Darcy opened and closed her mouth for a second like a fish in water.

'I can't believe you'd do this for me. Are you honestly sure Harvey doesn't mind? I don't want to be responsible for the reason he'd divorce you after the reception.'

'Honestly, it's all fine and dandy. Harvey wasn't always rich, mind you. You do know he's an East End boy at heart?'

'Is he really? Well, I be damned. I don't know how to thank you for this. You may have just saved my grandma's Lily's pub.'

'*Your* pub now, don't forget. Three generations of the Tanner women, which has to be something to celebrate, right?' She raised her glass before taking a sip.

'And that reminds me. I found some old postcards of my great Nan's during the war. So, I was thinking of turning this into a 1940s theme bar. What do you say?'

'I say it's fantastic. I wouldn't mind having a 1940s themed wedding, too.'

'Yeah?'

'Yeah, let's go for it.'

Jess was hovering around the table. 'I could design the dress. In fact, I've got something I've already started that would be suitable.' She put two glasses on the table.

Surprised to hear this news, Trudy looked at Darcy, a flash of confusion on her face.

'Trudy, this is Jess, my barmaid and fashion designer extraordinaire.'

Trudy stuck out her hand. 'Are you? Well, I might just take you up on that. We've only got a few weeks mind.'

'I may already have something that may interest you. I'll fetch it around tomorrow if that's okay with you.'

'What happened to the dresses you picked out?' Darcy asked. 'You've spent a fortune on them.'

Trudy waved her hand. 'Don't worry about them. The more I look at them the more I see what's wrong with them. Maybe having something designed, a one-off, is what I should've gone for in the first place.'

'I've never known a bride to leave the dresses so late.'

'You know how fussy I am. No, I'm happy with something original.'

'Well that's that then,' Darcy raised her glass to toast. 'And talking of World War Two, I found the key to the attic. Fancy coming up to have a look?'

'Yeah, come on.' Trudy drained the rest of her wine and rose to her feet.

As they went around the bar, Mr. Jones shouted for them to be careful. 'I don't want you coming through the roof now, ladies. Be careful.'

'We will,' Darcy shouted behind her as they made their way out of the bar.

Darcy got a chair from the kitchen, climbed on it and reached to open the lock.

The door swung open, spitting dust everywhere. She pulled the ladder down and jumped down from the chair, coughing and spluttering. 'Why do I always get the worst jobs?'

'Just a minute,' Trudy said and went to get her handbag. She came back wearing a scarf over her head. 'I've just had it dyed and I don't want dust settling in it.'

'You're looking the part of a 40's housewife,' Darcy laughed and climbed up the ladder. She poked her head around into the cool darkness. 'Yeah, I think I'll need a torch. I think there's one in the sideboard, will you pass me it?'

Trudy handed her the torch and she flicked it on, panning the beam of light around the room.

'What's up there?'

'Boxes and boxes of stuff.' She pulled herself up. 'I can't believe my father never came up here.'

She pulled the closest box towards her and then handed it to Trudy. 'Take this in the living room. I'll see what else I can find.'

She got down on all fours and put the torch in her mouth, yanking another box close and spat out the torch. 'Hey, I've found a box full of 40's clothes, too. I bet they're full of moth holes, though.'

'Any wedding dresses?'

'We should be so lucky. Here,' she passed her down another. 'Let's have a rummage through these first.' She got down and brushed the dust off her top. 'Find anything interesting?' She joined her on the rug.

'Darcy!' Trudy exclaimed, excitedly wiping the dust off a picture frame. 'Why on earth was this kept in the attic? I think you have a piece of history right here.' She turned the frame around revealing a black and white picture. Darcy leaned in for a closer look and gasped with shock. The picture was of Winston Churchill and a woman that looked like it could be her great grandmother standing behind the bar.

'So, the legend was true. He did come here.' She took the photograph. 'I need to find somewhere to hang this,' she said, excitedly.

Chapter Six

Standing behind the bar, swaying her hips to Glenn Miller's *In the Mood* that blasted from the speakers, Darcy received a notification on her phone. She picked it up from under the bar to find an email confirmation from the window repairman. He said he would be around in the week but would call her to confirm the time.

'We're getting there slowly,' she said to Mr. Jones sitting by the bar reading the sports section of the newspaper.

'Well, that's good news.' He looked behind him. 'And you have a few new customers, I see.'

'Yeah, I think most of them are students from Gareth's college,' she replied, wiping a glass from the towel slung over her shoulder.

'Where is he?'

'He's supposed to come by later. He said he wanted to look at the postcards with me.'

'Really?'

'Yeah. He's a history professor. I mean, what are the odds in me renting the flat to a history professor?'

'Stranger things have happened,' Mr. Jones replied. He straightened out his newspaper, grinning from ear to ear.

'I think it's such a romantic story though, isn't it? Tragic too. I wonder if my gran ever thought about him after she married my grandpa.'

'Probably did. We never forget the people we love, do we? Even if we've moved on to someone new.'

'True that.' She thought about her ex and blinked the image away when Gareth walked into the pub. She didn't want to think about Scott. Not after what he had put her through. He had told her that he loved her, and what he did was a stupid mistake. But more than once wasn't a mistake. How could he love her if he was cheating on her? She felt like an idiot, believing all the lies about working late.

The students cheered his arrival. Somewhat embarrassed, he walked up to the bar, putting his rucksack down on the empty stool. He nodded hello to Mr. Jones and took a seat.

'I see they took my advice on the excellent service, then.' He thumbed behind him.

'Thanks so much, I appreciate it.'

'No bother. Just don't tell them I live upstairs,' he laughed. 'Can I grab a pint?'

Darcy felt her heart quicken. 'Sure,' she reached to the top shelf for a clean glass, aware his eyes were still on her. 'I'm glad you popped in actually. I have something to show you that you'll be interested in.'

'Oh yeah?' His interest was piqued.

She handed him his pint and took the picture off the shelf. 'I found this in the attic earlier.'

Gareth was taken aback. 'Jesus! Sorry, pardon my language, will you? This is extraordinary. I have never seen this picture of Churchill before.' He pointed to the picture at the woman standing next to him. 'And this is your grandmother?'

'Yes, my great grandmother, the one who wrote the postcards. It's mad to think she didn't even have my gran at that point.'

'Amazing,' he said to himself, looking closely at the photo. 'Mind if I snap a picture of it with my phone? I'm sure my colleagues will be interested.'

'Sure.'

'It must be why she called it *The Churchill*,' he said, handing it back to her.

'I never thought of that,' she exclaimed. 'I was only pondering that very question this morning while I was cleaning the windows.'

'I thought there was something different about them when I passed,' he joked.

'Oh, *thank you.*' She took the tea-towel and playfully swiped him across the arm.

'While I'm here, can I have a look at the postcards, too? I may be able to help in tracing the fellow your gran was involved with.'

'Of course. So, you really like your history, huh?'

'Absolutely.'

'Well there's a heap more stuff back there you can look at later. I went up to the attic and found boxes of stuff from World War Two.'

'Really? Oh, I'd love that. I'll tell you what. How about I'll pick us up some food from the takeaway when you've finished here, and we can look at it together. Is that okay?'

Darcy saw Mr. Jones smirk behind his pint glass and rolled her eyes at him. 'That's fine.'

'Chinese, okay?'

'Perfect. Just tell them you know me, and they'll knock off twenty percent,' she laughed. 'I practically lived there when I first arrived and now they're like family.'

Gareth laughed.

Darcy rang the bell for the last orders and checked on her takings for the day.

'I think we did alright,' said Jess. 'We had a coach group in while you were sorting through the attic. I meant to tell you.'

'Brilliant. That reminds me too, I found a load of old forties clothes upstairs if you're interested in them. They're no good to me.'

'Do you mean that? Oh wow, thanks, Darcy. I'll look tomorrow if that's alright, or I'll miss my bus.'

'Sure,' she said and went back to totting up the total on the calculator.

'I have an idea,' Jess said excitedly. 'Why don't we go the full hog and wear forties clothes behind the bar? It'll give it a more authentic feel when it's transformed.'

Darcy thought for a moment and nodded her approval. 'Splendid. I love that idea. Okay then, we'll do that starting tomorrow.' She held out her hand. 'Let's shake on it. We make a good team.'

'Great. I'll bring the designs around for Trudy. I've already adjusted it as we're short on time, so I hope she approves.'

'Trust me. She will. In fact, she has no bloody choice anyway, changing her plans so late.'

Jess laughed.

'Right, I'm off,' said Mr. Jones, already standing by the door.

'Alright, Mr. Jones, see you tomorrow,' she waved.

He waved them goodnight and left.

'He's a strange fellow, isn't he?' said Jess, thoughtfully.

'Yes,' Darcy thought. 'He is a bit, but in a good way.'

'Do you even know anything about him besides he likes drinking Guinness?'

'Not really. Come to think of it, I don't even know where he lives. He was here the first day I arrived from Swansea. How he knew the pub was going to be open is anyone's guess.'

'Was he? Maybe it's his old haunt, bless him, and he couldn't wait to come back?'

'Possibly. I must find out one day.'

'Goodnight, Darcy, see you tomorrow night,' Jess said.

'Night, Jess and thanks,' she replied, thinking about what she had said. 'His old haunt? Nah.'

Darcy closed the door, locked up and switched off the lights, and as she turned to go back to her living quarters, there was a knock at the door. It was then she remembered that Gareth was calling around and turned back.

'Who is it?' she asked, to be sure.

'Gareth.'

'One moment,' she yelled and undid the latch and bolt on the door.

'Sorry, I'm late.' He stepped inside, carrying a plastic bag with the takeaway. 'I thought you'd forgotten when I realised the door was locked,' he laughed. 'I didn't fancy eating all this to myself.' He held up the bag as he brushed past her in the darkness.

'No bother, come through. And something smells nice.'

'Oh, thank you, I do my best,' he joked, pretending to sniff under his armpits. 'No, I wasn't sure what you liked, so I got a bit of everything.'

'Great, come through and take a seat.' She took him through to the living room and gestured to the sofa. 'Welcome to my home, I guess.' She sat down on her grandmother's chair next to the window.

Gareth removed his jacket and set it down on the arm of the sofa. 'Thanks. Still has its 1940's charm, I see.'

'My gran, Dad's mother, wasn't the type who liked decorating. She was always busy with the pub and everything else fell by the wayside.'

'So, you're happy here then, I take it?' he asked with keen interest as he served the rice onto the plates.

Darcy nodded, opened the wine and poured it into glasses. 'Yes. I've been here two months now. My Dad wasn't keen on coming back to London and asked if I wanted to take over the pub instead. It was that or put it up for sale.'

He handed her a plate. 'So, you've always been in the industry?'

Darcy laughed. 'No. I was working as a chef in a local hotel, and as luck would have it, my contract ended, so I decided to accept his offer without giving it much thought. I just packed a few bags and hopped on the train. Just like my great nan who came from Wales just before the war started.'

'On the subject of your great grandmother, do you have the postcards?' he asked, wiping his hands on a napkin.

'Yeah, just here,' she reached to the sideboard. 'Is history something you've always liked to study? I mean, you don't look like the typical history geeks I've known...'

He laughed. 'Is it my hair? My clothes?' he joked. 'We come in all shapes and fashions these days. But yeah, history has always fascinated me, especially World War Two. My mother was a teacher, in fact, she was a secondary school history teacher. So, I suppose you could say it also runs in the family.'

'So where are you from? If you don't mind me asking.'

'Dorset. I studied in London though, and since then I took a teaching post here and there. I haven't found a permanent position yet. In fact, this job came at the last minute. I've just finished my doctorate and was reluctant to take it as I couldn't find anywhere to live. I don't know whether it was luck or fate, but a friend of mine sent me your details and here we are.'

'Oh, right. So that's why you're only here for three months?'

'Yep, and then I move on until I can get somewhere permanent. It would be nice to settle down into a routine.' He went through the postcards, jotting down notes. 'I think it'll be nice to find out what became of...' he checked the name on the card again. 'Walter.' He looked at Darcy for approval.

'Definitely. It's such a shame they never met on Christmas Eve. It's so romantic...'

'Perhaps... no, doesn't matter,' he shrugged, pushing around rice on his plate.

'What?'

'I thought, maybe you'd like to come to the war rooms with me sometime in the week. Don't worry, it won't be a date or anything...' he said. 'Well, it could be...' He blushed.

Darcy shied away and focused on her plate of food, feeling her cheeks flush just a little. 'You know, I haven't been there yet. So, okay, yeah. I think it would be nice.'

'Great. We can talk more about your grandmothers, see what you already know.'

Chapter Seven

Sitting in the cold, empty bar, Darcy switched on her laptop before she opened the pub for the day with an idea to bring the pub into the twenty-first century. She opened her Facebook page and created a business page for the pub now it was getting its much-needed repairs.

The Churchill, Paddington London.
A pub where history is alive.

She uploaded pictures of the pub's exterior and interior, and included the Churchill picture with her gran, hoping that it would entice people to come. She sat back, pleased with her efforts, and took a moment to sit and really appreciate what she had inherited. She looked at the bar, imagining the people who once stood there, and her gran behind chatting and serving them. How many of those people would still be alive today, she wondered.

A knock on the door snapped her out of her thoughts.

'Just a minute,' she hollered and went to open the door, half expecting it to be Mr. Jones.

Gareth stood on the doorstep. 'Sorry, I know it's early...'

'That's okay. You could've just used the other door,' she laughed.

'I'll remember that next time. I just wanted to tell you I've paid you this month's rent.'

'Thanks. Do you want to come inside?'

'I must get to work. We'll catch up later, yeah? I may have news on our Walter. I went through the war records online after we spoke last night.'

'Brilliant, I'm excited to hear more, so I'll see you later then.' She waved him off as he walked down the street.

'Taken a shine to him, I see?'

Darcy jumped back. 'Mr. Jones, you bloody scared me then. Where did you come from?' She looked up and down the busy street. 'I'm not open yet, but oh okay, seeing as it's you, come on in and I'll pop the kettle on.'

'Any biscuits?' he asked cheekily.

'I'll have a look.'

BEFORE SHE OPENED, Darcy went into her living quarters and rummaged through the pile of clothes she had found and washed, hoping to find something that would fit her. She found a blouse and a skirt and then pinned her hair in victory rolls. She stood back from the mirror to appraise her appearance, thinking Trudy would approve of her new style as she always moaned at her for wearing jeans.

When she went out to the bar, Mr. Jones and Jess, who had just walked in to start her shift, gasped.

'You look stunning, Darcy. But don't forget the classic red lips. Here.' She rummaged through her bag. 'I have a red lip liner you can borrow.'

'Gosh, that takes me back,' said Mr. Jones thoughtfully.

'You looked the part yourself,' she joked, thinking that she hadn't seen him wear anything different over the past couple of months. *How strange.* 'So, Jess, did you design the clothes yourself?' she asked.

'No, I found these in a charity shop on my way to college yesterday.' She twirled around.

There was a tap at the door, and Darcy looked up.

'I've come to sort out your windows, love,' said a man standing in the doorway wearing overalls that were stained with splotches of different coloured paint.

'Okay, great. Thank you.'

'It's getting there. So, what are you going to do about Christmas?' asked Mr. Jones.

'One thing at a time,' she said, noticing the delivery van outside. 'I'm too busy to even think about Christmas, Mr. Jones.' She walked to the bar to greet the driver at the door.

The afternoon brought more customers into the pub. Darcy was busy wiping glasses behind the bar when the man that came in with the group walked over and introduced himself.

'Darcy, isn't it?'

'Yes, that's right. How can I help?'

He produced a business card. 'I'm Jack from the *Daily News*. I write for the entertainment section, and I saw on Facebook that you're planning an opening night here?'

'Yes, that's right for my World War Two re-opening'.

'Brilliant. It sounds like something I'd like to write an article about. Is that okay with you?'

'Really?' She took the card. 'That's great. Do you want to do an interview or...'?

'Sure, perhaps we could arrange a suitable time?'

'Pop along to the re-opening tomorrow. I'm sure I could spare a few minutes.'

'Great, I'll see you then.'

She swung around. 'You never guess what?' she squealed to Jess. 'We've got the interest of the local paper.'

'That's excellent, Darcy. Trudy has shown up, too. She's over there.' She pointed to the table.

'Great, while it's quiet, we'll sort out the wedding, come on.' She grabbed a few glasses and filled them with wine and brought them over to the table.

'Drinking your stock, eh?' Trudy said, taking a glass. 'So, have you got the dress?'

'Here,' she said, taking her drawing pad out of her folder, and passed it to Trudy.

Darcy waited with anticipation as she watched Trudy frown, then smile, and then pursed her lips.

'I love it. You have a gift. I don't know why I didn't think of hiring a designer.'

'That's a relief, so we're set for the 24th then?'

'Yes. By the way, who was that you were speaking to just now?'

'A reporter from the *Daily News*. He's coming to write an article about the pub tomorrow night.'

'I told you things would work out, didn't I?'

Darcy saw a few people come into the pub and rose to her feet. She had a lot of work to do before it was ready for the opening night. 'I'd best get to work then, speak to you later.'

Darcy brought out a box of her grandmother's things and set it on the bar. 'Right, I think it's time to bring the past alive, then.' She hung the picture of Churchill and her gran on the wall next to the piano. 'Mr. Jones, do you know anyone who can play this?' She opened the lid and played *Jingle Bells*. 'I only know this song.'

'I think everyone knows how to play that song,' laughed Jess.

'There was a lad who used to drink here that played. I'm not sure if he still lives around here now. Why don't you stick a notice in the window for someone?'

Darcy smiled. 'What would I do without you here for the past couple of months, eh?'

There were footsteps behind her, and she glanced over her shoulder, surprised to see Gareth.

'Finished early?' she asked.

He came towards the piano and gently slipped her hand away from the keys. 'Yeah, short day today. So, did I hear you needed a piano player?' he asked and then sat down on the stool.

'Someone who can play more than *Jingle Bells*,' she laughed as she watched him break into a rendition of '*We'll Meet Again.*'

Darcy leaned against the piano, with one arm propped on the top as she watched his long fingers glide over the keys. She caught him looking her way a few times and realised that she was catching feelings for him.

'I could play a few nights. That's if you want me too?' he offered. 'I won't charge you.' He winked.

'Would you really? It'll only be until I can find someone permanent. Thank you.'

'Anytime. It beats sitting upstairs on my own.'

'I'll get you a drink, on the house.' She returned to the bar, cheeks flushed and heart pounding against her chest.

'Someone's in love,' Jess said when she returned to the bar.

'Shush, he can hear you,' she whispered. 'And no...' Darcy stopped herself, shrugged it off and went to collect a glass from the bar. 'Okay, you win. Maybe I like him, but he's only here for a while and then he's off on another job. Besides, I don't even know if he has a girlfriend.'

'You're going to the War Rooms this afternoon, aren't you? So, ask him then. But I highly doubt it, Darcy. Look at him,' she nodded towards him. 'Since he's been here, I've noticed he only has eyes for you.'

Darcy slapped her hand on her forehead. 'I forgot I was going. Are you alright to cover for me?'

'Of course, I told you. But how on earth could you forget you had a date with him?'

'This place has been running me ragged.'

Roll out the Barrel rang out around the room. Darcy looked in his direction, and at the same time, Gareth lifted his head and smiled at her. 'You're right,' she said to Jess and went to pour him a drink.

'Right about what?' she asked, confused.

Chapter Eight

The song ended, and a rapturous applause broke out in the room. Gareth got up from his seat, mockingly bowed and went to the bar. Darcy wondered if her hair looked all right and knew then that there was no way back. She had fallen for him. And that scared her. She didn't know if she was ready to feel that way again about someone. Let alone being with someone.

'Are you ready for our...' he paused, seemingly thinking of the appropriate word.

'Day out?' Darcy offered.

'Yes. A day out,' he then smiled.

'Give me two minutes,' she replied.

There wasn't much time to change her clothes, so she grabbed her coat from her living room and went to join Gareth at the bar. He was sitting next to Mr. Jones, talking, and just as she walked through the doorway, he looked up with a huge smile on his face. 'Well, you look the part.' He rose from his seat. 'I thought we'd take the tube, is that alright?'

'Fine with me.' She picked up her handbag from under the bar. 'Will you be okay?' She turned to Jess pulling a pint.

'Of course. Now off you go.'

'I could always lend a hand if things get busy,' said Mr. Jones.

'Oh. Thank you, that'd be great.'

There was a cold nip in the air when she stepped out of the pub.

Gareth fell in step with her, and they walked down towards the tube station.

'Have a good day today?' she asked.

'I did.' He pulled his mobile out of his jacket pocket 'I also managed to find something out about our Walter, too.'

He passed her the phone. 'He was in the 1st Battalion and was quite the hero, too.'

'Shame we don't have a picture, isn't it?'

'I'm working on it. A friend of mine back home does family research in his spare time, so I have him looking further into it.'

'I hope it's no trouble. I mean, I'd look myself if I knew where to start.'

'No, no trouble at all.' He offered her his arm. Darcy linked his arm and they headed to the underground station.

'Thanks for agreeing to play for us. Any more talents that we should know about?' Darcy laughed while she stood at the ticket machine. She took her purse out of her bag, but Gareth stepped in with his card. 'No, I'd like to do this. It's my treat today. What about you?' he asked, heading to the turnstiles. 'I bet there's more to you than pulling pints and cooking.'

'Well you know I can't play the piano, but I've sung professionally in my time.'

The train slowed to a stop and the doors slid open.

'After you,' he said. 'Maybe we could be a duo. You sing and me on the piano?'

The train was heaving with people. They stood in the aisle and held on to the overhead rail. It jerked slightly as it moved, slamming Darcy into Gareth. She caught a whiff of his scent, *Paco Raban*, which only added to his allure. She had to get a hold of herself. His hand wrapped around her on impact, and when she moved, she felt his hand slowly glide across her back to her hip.

'Sorry,' she stood back, getting a firmer grip on the bar.

His eyes crinkled with laughter. 'Quite all right. Glad I could be of service.'

They exited the tube at Westminster just as Big Ben chimed. A red double decker passed as the clock struck two.

'Gosh, I haven't been here since I was a kid on an art school trip,' she enthused.

'What? You've been in London for two months and you've been stuck in Paddington all that time?'

Darcy nodded. 'Yeah,' she stuck her hands in her coat pockets. 'I've been so busy getting it clean and ready for the opening. I had no choice, really. It has to pay off, but as you've seen it's been a slow start.' She just hoped it would start picking up after the opening.

'You've pulled it together though. I think the forties' theme will do very well. It seems to be the thing lately, what with novels and what have you. So, I heard you want someone to play piano regularly?' he asked, genuinely interested.

'Why? Looking for a permanent job, are you?' she laughed, thinking he couldn't be serious.

'Who knows?' he shrugged. 'I don't have a job after this one, so I'll have to go back home to Dorset for a while.'

'With your girlfriend or...?' she inquired, then regretted being so brash.

Gareth smirked.

'No, I'm single. You?' He playfully nudged her arm.

'Got a girlfriend, you mean?' she joked. 'No, I haven't long come out of a long-term relationship. He was bad news, unfortunately, such a shame I didn't figure it out sooner.'

'Sorry to hear that. Some men don't know what they've got even when it's staring them in the face.'

'His loss. I mean, I doubt I would ever have come to London if we were still together, so he did me a favour.' She shrugged, walking down the street passing the parliament buildings to the right.

They came to the curb, waiting to cross the road. Big Ben chimed two o'clock and Darcy looked up like an excited child. 'Do you remember that on the news, or am I showing my age?'

'You're showing your age,' he laughed. 'No, I must be around your age. Thirty-five?'

'Thirty-four.'

They crossed the road when a woman bumped into Darcy, knocking her sideways into Gareth. Their hands brushed against one another's and just as Darcy was about to apologise to him, he took her hand.

'Is that okay?' he asked, staring into her eyes.

She half expected him to crack a joke, but it wasn't forthcoming. Her heart pounded in her chest. 'Yeah, it's fine,' she replied, now feeling her cheeks flush hot with embarrassment. Was this turning into a date? she wondered.

They reached the opposite side of the road and walked towards the War Rooms. Gareth went to the glass booth and bought the tickets.

'Ready?' he asked.

'Yes, I just hope they don't mistake me as part of the exhibition.'

Chapter Nine

'Wow, did we win the war?' Jess asked as she walked into the pub for her afternoon shift.

Darcy strained to reach the bunting above the window and flopped down on the seat, sweating and exhausted. She sat back to catch her breath as she looked around the pub at all her hard work. Union Jack buntings hung behind the bar and across the ceiling, and her grandmother's gas mask hung on the post next to black and white pictures of VE day she had printed off the internet.

Darcy felt proud. 'Yeah,' she nodded at her efforts. 'It looks like we did, eh?' She turned to Jess, still standing in the doorway, gawping at all the bits and pieces Darcy had put up. 'Jesus, what did you do to your hair?' She rose to her feet, fascinated by the multi-coloured stripes of hair.

'It's called unicorn hair; do you like it?' She gave it a flick off her shoulder.

'Gosh, yeah, it's absolutely stunning. Wish I had the guts to go to that extreme.'

Jess laughed and went to the bar. 'You should let me colour it for you one day.'

Darcy shook her head. 'Oh no, I'm not as bold as you youngsters.' She picked a box up from the floor and went through its contents.

'Not bold, did you say? Aren't you the one who went on a date with her tenant yesterday afternoon?'

'It wasn't a date,' Darcy shrugged. Although she admitted it had felt like a date, and she wished it had been. She couldn't wipe the smile off her face, and Jess caught on.

'Admit you like him, come on.'

Darcy's smile slowly disappeared, and she put down the picture she held of her grandmother and her as a child. 'He's only here temporarily. Wouldn't it be foolish of me to get involved with someone who will be leaving just after Christmas?' She shook her head, on the verge of tears. 'I don't want to get hurt. Again,' she said softly. She picked up the box and went into her living quarters. While she wiped the smudged mascara off her face, Jess appeared by the door.

'Sorry, Darcy, I didn't mean...'

'No, no, it's not you, honestly. I think I'm just so tired.' She looked in the mirror hanging above the fireplace. 'I've got the reporter coming soon, so I'd better clean up in case he wants to take pictures,' she chuckled.

'Alright, well, the pub is starting to get packed, so you never know, word about this place may have already got out.'

Darcy put on her flower-patterned tea dress and gave her lips another coat of red lipstick. She felt proud of what she'd achieved so far as she stepped out into the bar that hadn't seen so much life in a long time. She instantly went to serve a customer.

'What can I get you?' Darcy asked over the chatter and music that had started on the piano. She looked to her side, and over several heads, she saw Gareth sitting at the piano playing *A Nightingale Sang in Berkeley Square.* Her heart melted.

'Excuse me,' she heard and then snapped back to what she was doing.

The reporter stood behind her customer, waving to get her attention. 'Sorry, I'll be with you in one moment.' She went back to serving the customer when another wanted a drink.

'I'll help, go and see the reporter,' said Mr. Jones, rolling up the sleeves of his white shirt.

'Thank you,' she patted his shoulder and stepped around.

She pulled out a chair at the table at the back of the room and then shook his hand. 'I didn't expect it to get this busy, I'm sorry about that.'

He waved a dismissive hand at her comment. 'This is what you wanted, isn't it?'

'Yes, it is.'

Darcy then proceeded to tell him how she acquires the pub and talked about the postcards she had found.

'Would you mind if I take a picture of you and your staff?' He looked in the direction of the piano and called Gareth over. Before Darcy could explain that he wasn't staff, the reporter already had them in a comfortable position and was snapping away. 'Thank you.' He gave them the thumbs up. 'Could you move a little closer,' he instructed Darcy who was now touching shoulders with Gareth.

After several more camera flashes, the reporter thanked them and said to watch out for the weekend edition.

'Sorry about that,' she said to Gareth. 'He assumed you were staff.' She laughed.

'No harm was done and anyway, I quite enjoyed it. How about you come and sing a song with me when things quieten down?'

'You remembered?'

'I don't forget a thing, honey.' He winked and returned to the piano, where a small crowd had gathered.

Darcy went about clearing old glasses from the tables when Trudy and Harvey came in. 'Hello, you two. I didn't expect to see you here tonight.'

Harvey was a tall, broad-shouldered man with thinning blonde hair. Darcy referred to him as the big friendly giant. He gave Darcy a kiss on the cheek and then looked around the pub.

Darcy shot Trudy a worried look. Fearing she hadn't done enough in terms of repairs, she waited in anticipation for his verdict. There was no way she could afford to pay back four thousand pounds right now.

'It's...very nice, Darcy. I like what you've done.' He smiled.

Darcy let out a slow exhale. 'Thank God for that. So, it's good enough for your wedding reception?'

'Darcy, I know you think I'm a cold-hearted businessman, but relax, for crying out loud. I think you've got something good going here. And yes, I'm more than happy to have my wedding reception here.'

'Thanks, big man,' she said. 'Now I've got to go behind the bar, see you in a little while.'

'Darcy, Darcy...' everyone in the pub began chanting her name and wondered what was going on.

Gareth stood up from behind the piano. 'I think you owe us a song.' He started clapping, encouraging everyone else until she finally agreed.

'Just the one song, alright.'

He patted the stool next to him for her to sit down. 'How about *White Cliffs of Dover?*' He smiled cheekily and leaned in close. 'I heard you singing it yesterday,' he whispered and began playing the song. 'You really should close your bathroom window.'

Trying not to laugh, she began to sing, forgetting how much she enjoyed it. The song ended with a round of applause, and Gareth got her up to take a bow.

'Beautiful,' he whispered in her ear and then went to the bar.

She went to join Trudy and Harvey sat in a booth.

'That was wonderful,' Harvey raised his glass.

'So, what's going on with you two?' asked Trudy. She gave a nod to Gareth. 'Are you going to ask him to be your date to the wedding?'

'You could ask him to play the piano,' Harvey said.

'Good idea,' said Trudy. 'Do you think he would? We'll pay him, of course.'

Darcy didn't think she was serious for a moment, but then Trudy got up from her seat.

'I'm going to ask him.'

'No, wait,' Darcy followed her and dragged her back. 'He's leaving before Christmas.' She rolled her eyes.

'Like hell he is.'

'Darce, you did say it's alright if I have my fashion show here, didn't you? It's just that it's next week,' Jess asked, about to leave.

'Sure, of course. See you tomorrow,' she yawned and looked towards the piano where Gareth was still sat twinkling the ivories.

The last of the customers went, and she thanked Mr. Jones for his help.

'Would you like a job here?' she asked him, taking a twenty pound note out of the till. 'Here you go, for helping.'

'No, I couldn't possibly.'

Darcy insisted. 'Please, you really helped me tonight. So how about a little job?'

He thought for a moment. 'Alright, thank you. I really enjoyed it.'

'Yes, you're a natural, I saw you.'

'Well, I have dabbled with bar work before, but that was back in my younger days.' He picked up his jacket. 'I'll be off then, goodnight, all.' He waved.

'I must find a chance to ask him about his life one day,' she said to no one in particular.

She put the latch on and bolted the door and went to join Gareth at the piano.

'Thanks for tonight, too. I really appreciate it.'

He stopped playing and swung around to face her. 'To think I almost didn't take this job in London...' He brushed a ringlet of hair behind her ear.

She shivered at this touch and drew closer. 'I'm glad you did, but...'

He pressed a finger to her lips and reached in for a kiss.

Chapter Ten

'Okay, Mr. Jones, you win. Let's decorate for Christmas.' She dropped the box of decorations she had bought on the table. 'I'm hoping they'll be in keeping with the vintage feel of the pub, but fear not, I'm off shopping later…'

He gave her a questioning look. 'You're a lot chirpier, that's nice to see. Christmas was the best part of this pub. Your gran used to go all out with decorations…'

'Mr. Jones,' she interrupted him. 'Would you like a cup of tea before we open?'

'Yes, I wouldn't mind, thank you.'

Darcy went to her kitchen and made a pot of tea. She found a sticky toffee pudding in the cupboard and put that on a tray, too. 'Here we go,' she put it on the table and pulled out a chair. Mr. Jones joined her. 'You know,' she poured the tea. 'I've realised that I've been here three months now and we never had a proper chat about you.'

He brought the cup to his lips and then put it back down. 'I'm not a man of many words, Darcy. 'But ask away…'

'You knew both of my grans, and I never once asked you what your first name is or where you even lived around here. I feel terrible.'

'Oh, don't you worry about me, but yes, I knew your grans. They treated me well, they did. Every Sunday your grandmother Lily used to serve Sunday lunches here. They were the best this side of the Thames, I tell you.'

She noticed he avoided her question and felt she didn't want to prod any further. Some people didn't like to talk about their past, and she respected his decision.

'I never knew they served lunch here. Maybe it's something I ought to start again, eh? What do you think?' she asked, passing him a slice of cake.

'It's a splendid idea. Thanks for the tea and cake, it's really kind of you.'

'No bother.'

There was a knock at the door, and she went to answer it, thinking she may as well open for the day.

'One Christmas tree,' said a young man, checking his clipboard.

'Yes, could you fetch it in, thanks? Hey, Mr. Jones,' she yelled. 'We have a Christmas tree. Happy now?' she chuckled.

She moved a table and then went into the kitchen for a bucket to put it in. The delivery man called her. 'Is there a problem?' she asked, returning to the bar, staring at the rear end of the tree that was stuck in the doorway.

'You could say that.'

'I guess I should've measured the doors first,' she laughed, tugging the end of it. She pulled and pulled. Mr. Jones came to help, and then after several seconds, the tree came loose.

'Where do you want it?' he asked.

Darcy pointed to the empty space beside the piano. 'Would you mind?' she replied, helping him lift into the bucket.

WHILE SHE SERVED THE two customers that had come in, her phone pinged with a message. She handed over their change and took her phone out of her pocket. It was her mother.

'How are things going?' she asked.

'Good. I think I'm slowly turning things around. Why don't you and Dad come down to London for a break, see what I've done with the place?'

'It's why I'm calling, love. We'll be there for Christmas, alright? Trudy's mam is traveling down for the wedding, so she said your father and I can go with her.'

'Brilliant, I'll have to make some room…'

'Are you still renting out the flat?'

'Yeah, on a temporary basis until I can get on my feet.' She thought about Gareth and how he'd be leaving soon. 'Mam, it's getting busy here, so I'll speak to you later.'

'Yes, call me, Darcy. You rarely keep in touch these days.'

'Mam, it's been non-stop since I got here. You'll soon see.'

She ended the call and slipped her phone into the back of her jeans.

'Everything okay?' Jess asked.

'Yeah, it was my mother. She's coming for Christmas.' She rolled her eyes. 'I must make room for them somehow.' She took a damp rag from under the bar and went to wipe an empty table that had been vacated.

'I was going to say you shouldn't have let out the flat, but then we wouldn't have anyone to ogle over, would we?'

Darcy found her hilarious and went back to the bar, remembering she had to order the wedding food.

While she was sitting behind the bar on her laptop, scrolling through the options the website had to offer, she realised it was a lot of work for two people. 'I hope that's everything.' She hit send, confirming the order. 'I may have to hire a few more girls for the day.'

'I know a couple of people looking for a job.'

'Great, get them to call me.'

That evening, after she had locked up, she went to the bar and poured herself a drink. 'To me,' she raised herself a toast, thinking she hadn't seen Gareth all day. The clock struck 1.15 a.m. so she switched off the lights and went into her living room.

As she was dozing off on the sofa, she thought she heard her door knock. She got up and went to the pub. 'Who is it?'

'Gareth, I wondered if you wanted some company.'

She felt her stomach flutter and quickly opened the door. 'You must be freezing?' she said as he stepped inside.

He gave her a kiss on the cheek with his cool lips. 'Very.'

'Come through,' she said, leading the way.

'I'm sorry I didn't call around. I had to stay and help a few students with their end of term essays.'

At that moment, she felt a little silly for thinking he wasn't interested anymore. She switched on the lamp on the sideboard.

Gareth took off his coat. His jumper accentuated his muscular, trim frame.

Her eyes lingered longer than she intended. 'Would you like a hot drink?'

'If it's no bother,' he said and sat down on the sofa.

Darcy went to put the kettle on. 'Did you find out any more about Walter?' she enquired, spooning coffee into two mugs.

'My mate is on it. He said we should get something soon. Doesn't your grandmother know anything?'

'No,' she said, carrying the mugs into the living room. 'My gran passed away last year. As I was the only grand-daughter, I got the pub. Dad didn't want to take it on. In fact, he wanted to sell it.'

'You didn't, obviously, or you wouldn't be here.'

'At first, yes it did cross my mind about selling it. When I came here and saw what was involved, I wanted to hop on the next train back home, but I think nostalgia got the best of me in the end, so that's why I stuck it out for as long as I did.' She reached under the coffee table for a tin of chocolates she'd been saving and offered him one.

'And now you're a success.' He put the mug on the coffee table and joined her on the sofa.

'Hardly, but I guess I'm doing better than a few weeks ago. Do you want the TV on?' Darcy picked up the remote from the arm of the sofa.

'Sure,' he replied and put an arm around her.

Feeling comfortable in his presence, she slipped off her shoes and snuggled up to him.

'Darcy.' She felt someone shaking her. 'Wake up, you've been robbed.'

She snapped her eyes open and shot up, thinking she was having a nightmare.

'Darcy,' said Gareth. 'You left the door unlocked. I'm calling the police.'

She sprung off the sofa and dashed towards the pub.

'Don't touch anything,' Gareth yelled.

Standing in the bar, Darcy covered her mouth with her hands trying to take in the scene before her. Chairs and tables were overturned, glasses smashed along the bar and the floor, and the till was opened with all the takings gone. 'Why would someone do this?' She felt Gareth's arm wrapped around her.

'Police are on their way,' he sighed. 'I don't know why anyone would want to do something like this, but don't worry, it'll get sorted.'

The flashing blue lights of the police car shone through the window. Darcy took out her mobile from her pocket and texted her parents. Three police officers came into the pub asking to speak to Darcy.

She gave the officer all the information she could. It was four a.m. when the police left, and she couldn't face cleaning up. 'I'm just going to make a cup of coffee and...' A sob caught in her throat. Gareth pulled her in close.

'Do you want me to sleep on the sofa?' he whispered.

Darcy nodded. 'Please...'

Unable to sleep, Darcy threw her duvet off and went into the kitchen. She took a sweeping brush, only to find that everything had already been cleared.

'You didn't have to do that,' she said.

'It's the least I could do. I feel like if I didn't come around last night, you wouldn't have opened the door...'

'Don't be silly, it was my mistake. Besides, I enjoyed your company.' She began tying up the bin bags.

'Darcy, I need to talk to...'

Darcy heard her phone and pulled it out of her back pocket. 'Sorry, just a moment.' She accepted the call. 'Hi, Mam, yes.' She sat down on the stool. 'All the takings are gone, but there's not a lot of damage, thankfully.'

'Your Dad is on the way. He got the early train this morning, so expect him about eleven.'

'Alright, Mam, I'll speak to you later.'

'Everything okay?' asked Gareth, putting an arm around her shoulders.

'Yeah, my Dad is on the way.'

Chapter Eleven

At ten o' clock, Darcy opened the pub door and stood on the doorstep, watching the passing traffic.

'Penny for your thoughts,' said Jess, bounding up the pavement with a suitcase and an art folder.

Darcy exhaled. 'You'd better come in.'

'Has something happened?' She put her stuff on the table and removed her coat.

'We had a robbery last night. They took all the takings and smashed a few things...'

Jess gave Darcy a hug. 'I can't believe it. How did they get in?'

'The door.' She shook her head, thinking how stupid she had been. 'I more or less invited them in.'

'What?'

Darcy pulled out a chair. 'Gareth came around after closing, so when I answered, I forgot to lock it again.'

'So, you are opening today, I take it?' Jess pulled out a chair and sat down.

'I can't afford not to open today. The police said they be in touch later.' She rose to her feet. 'Oh, and my Dad is coming. He'll be here at eleven.'

Jess jumped to her feet. 'I know it's not the right time then, but I have some of my designs here I'd like to run past you if you have a minute this afternoon.'

Darcy smiled. 'Of course, and that reminds me. I'd better get out of these jeans and put my war outfit on, as they say, keep calm and carry on.'

'Things are only sent to try us, right?'

'Absolutely. No point dwelling right now; I've come too far to let a bunch of idiots win.'

Darcy was down the cellar, having just changed a barrel when she heard Jess calling her.

'There's a guy here to see you.'

Dad.

Excited to see him, she closed the cellar door and walked into the pub to find him already behind the bar, pulling pints. He was dressed in his usual leather jacket and ripped jeans.

'Hey, Dad.'

'Darce, my girl, how are you?' He came around the bar, wrapping his arms around her in a tight hug.

'I'm alright, Dad, just a bit crushed, like.'

He let her go. 'Sorry, love. So, what happened? Have they caught the buggers yet?' He took off his jacket revealing a band t-shirt and sleeve tattoos.

Darcy shook her head. 'Not yet. Just hope the insurance will cover it,' she sighed. 'Jess, this is my dad, Dylan. Dad, this is Jess and Mr. Jones, who I told you about.'

'Yes, we've already met. Thanks for being there for my girl.' He shook hands with Mr. Jones sitting by the bar.

'My pleasure.'

'Right, Darcy, if you want to take a little break, do some shopping or whatever, I can hold the fort.'

'But you've only just got here.' She noticed the pub had become quite busy. 'Isn't the article in the paper today, Jess?'

'Yes, it is. Do you want me to go next door for a few copies?'

'Would you mind?'

'What's going on?' Dylan asked.

'We had an article printed about us,' she beamed. 'Pictures and everything.'

Moments later, Jess walked into the pub clutching a pile of newspapers and set them down on the bar. 'Here you go.' She passed everyone a copy. 'Page four.'

They all snatched a copy and flicked over the pages. Darcy held up the paper for the customers to see. 'Have you seen this?' she asked, excitedly.

There was a round of applause. Darcy took a bow and went to switch on the music from her iPod.

'No Bakelite radio, then, you know for authenticity?' Her father laughed cheekily.

'We have a piano player. Well, except he's not permanent...'

'It's her boyfriend, Mr. Tanner,' said Jess, passing to get to the other side of the bar.

'Dylan, please. So, who is the lucky fella, and I'm going to meet him, right?'

'He's in the picture,' she pointed. 'And I don't think we're official yet, so don't go embarrassing me.'

Later that afternoon, Darcy and Jess sat around the table covered with drawings.

'So, this is what I plan on doing,' said Jess. 'It helps with my overall mark, plus it'll bring in plenty of students.'

Darcy liked the idea very much. 'That's great, so we'll just move a few tables here, so your models can walk out of the toilets, sorry, changing rooms, and they walk up the runway here,' she pointed. 'Brilliant. So, we're sorted for Tuesday, right?'

'Thanks, Darcy, and I'll bring Trudy's dress around in the morning, I think she'll love it.'

Darcy made a start on collecting the empty glasses while Vera Lynn played in the background.

'Darcy,' her father called. 'You're looking tired, love. Why don't you go and take a break? I'm fine here.'

'You are looking tired, your Dad's right, take a break,' Mr. Jones said.

Darcy couldn't argue with them. She had only managed an hour's kip after the break-in.

'I wouldn't mind.' She put the empty glasses on the bar, feeling safer now that her dad was here to oversee things.

Darcy woke to a sing-along taking place in the bar. Her dad was quite the party animal, so she wasn't sure why she was so surprised.

She opened the door to see everyone enjoying themselves. She saw her father and Gareth chatting at the end of the bar. Gareth saw her and waved.

'You didn't say your boyfriend lived upstairs.'

Gareth laughed into his drink.

'I see you've been introduced, then?'

'I have some news about our Walter,' Gareth said. 'And Mr. Jones over there,'

'What's going on?' asked Dylan.

Darcy stepped in.

'When I came here, I found postcards written by great nana, Lily, to a gentleman during the war. They were supposed to meet on Christmas Eve at Piccadilly Circus, but he didn't turn up. So, what did you find out about Mr. Jones?' she asked eagerly.

'Come over here, both of you,' he said and walked around to the quietest part of the bar.

'Well, I found out that Walter came from the West Country, near to where I live, actually. So, I got my mate on the case for you. But what I really wanted to talk to you about was Mr. Jones.'

'Well I hope it's nothing bad,' Darcy said and looked across the bar at him serving a customer.

'No, quite the opposite, in fact. So, I did a thorough check on the pub and its history while I was at work, and I don't know why but I've been curious about him for a while. Anyway, I did a background check and Mr. Jones is actually mentioned several times. His name is Samuel, and he was adopted out of the family by... your father's mother.'

Dylan put down his pint in shock. 'Are you sure about this? I never knew. My mother never said she had another son.'

'It might never have been spoken about. In those days, it probably wasn't,' Gareth replied. 'She was sixteen when she had him.'

'Bloody hell!' Darcy whispered, staring at Mr. Jones who was oblivious to the conversation taking place. 'It's no wonder he knows everything. Gosh... I don't know what to say to him now.'

'Just be your normal self,' said Gareth. 'If he wanted a fuss made, well, I guess he would've said or done something by now.'

'That's true,' Dylan said.

'What do we do, Dad? Do we go and talk to him?'

'The sooner the better. Let me finish my pint first; I need it.'

Astounded, Darcy called over Jess and Trudy, who had just walked in. She explained the situation to them and asked if they'd watch the pub for a while.

'I'd better go and talk to the man,' said Dylan, taking a deep breath before he tapped him on the shoulder. 'Mr. Jones, do you mind if we have a word?'

Darcy suggested they'd go into the living room while she made a pot of coffee.

'Am I being sacked?' he asked, confused as he sat down.

Darcy brought out the coffee pot and three cups and set them down on the table.

'No,' she said and looked at her father. 'Do you want to tell him or shall I?'

'I will,' he cleared his throat. 'Why didn't you tell us you were family?' he asked, choked with emotion.

Mr. Jones looked at Darcy and then back at Dylan. 'You know? But how?'

Darcy sat on the arm of the chair. 'Gareth found out while he was doing some research for me. I think it's wonderful, don't you Dad?' she replied.

Dylan nodded. The tears welled in his eyes, and he wiped them away with his sleeve. 'You didn't have to keep quiet. I'm sure our mother would've wanted us to get to know each other.'

Mr. Jones took a handkerchief out of his trouser pocket and wiped his eyes. 'I'm so happy, you know. I just couldn't find a way to tell you. Mum gave me to her cousin to take care of me, so I was always around the family. Except I didn't know she was our mum until I turned eighteen, and by that time, she left London to start her new life with your father.'

'Why didn't she ever tell me about you?' Dylan asked.

'It was agreed way back then to keep it quiet. I don't know, times were different then.'

'Well, I'm sure as hell happy I know now, come here,' Dylan rose to his feet and pulled Mr. Jones in for a hug.

Darcy was too emotional to speak, but everything that had happened over the last month suddenly made sense to her.

DARCY HEADED BACK TO the pub, looking for Gareth.

'Are you okay?' asked Jess, noticing that she had been crying.

'I'll explain in a minute,' she replied and fell into Gareth's open arms.

'I missed you today,' he said. 'I was worried about you after what happened – you are alright now, are you?'

'I'm okay, yeah. I think I remember you wanted to talk about something this morning. What was it?'

'Do you have a minute?' he nodded to the quiet booth.

'Sure,' she turned to her dad who had emerged from the living room with Mr. Jones. 'I won't be a minute.'

'It's alright, love. Take all the time you need.'

Gareth took her hand, pulling her to him. 'When I came to London, I didn't expect to meet anyone as special as you. To be honest, I didn't want to fall too deeply because I knew I was leaving, but...I can't help it. I think I'm falling in love with you.'

'I love you, too, but let's not talk about you leaving yet. We'll cross that bridge when we come to it.'

'Meet me tomorrow after work?' Gareth asked.

'I'm meeting Trudy on Oxford Street, so if you want to meet me afterward, say six?'

Chapter Twelve

Linking arms to keep warm, Darcy and Trudy strolled down a busy Oxford Street admiring the Christmas window displays. She planned on getting her Christmas presents sorted today so she could concentrate on the pub, but they were having so much fun taking in the Christmas spirit and decorations. A large crowd had gathered around a shop window, and they stopped to take a look.

'All set for the wedding next week?' asked Darcy, pulling out her phone to snap a picture of the snowmen in the window.

'Can't wait, babe,' her lips chattered in the cold. 'Shall we get a coffee somewhere? I really need to warm up.'

'Yeah, that's a brilliant idea. I'm frozen.'

They began walking again. 'So how did your father take the news about Mr. Jones?'

'He was shocked at first, as was I, but he came around to the idea pretty quick. I mean, what else could he say or do?'

'It's all rather strange though, isn't it? I know I'm not the brightest spark in the box, but doesn't it seem like all this has been orchestrated? You've got a World War Two historian staying with you...'

'Oh, don't be daft,' Darcy laughed. 'But Gareth is supposed to be leaving after Christmas, and I don't know what to do. I've already fallen for him.'

'Oh, come on, Darce, I think I knew this before you even realised it yourself.'

Trudy pointed to Starbucks, and they walked in, grateful for the warmth. After they had ordered, they sat at a table beside the window.

'He's a great guy, Darcy. Maybe you can both find a way to make it work, huh?'

'I hope so. I'm meeting him after this.'

Darcy noticed Trudy's face drained of colour. 'Don't look now but there's Scott. I'm not even joking, Darcy.'

'What the hell would he be doing here?' asked Darcy. 'And in this part of London too,' she laughed and glanced behind her. Standing in the queue was Scott. 'Oh no, Trude, how can this be? London is humungous, and I happen to see him?'

'Harvey has opened a new office close to here. I didn't want to tell you.'

'Crap, so you brought me here knowing his office is only a few streets away. He can't see us, right?' She covered the side of her face with her hand.

A worried look crossed Trudy's face.

'Don't tell me...'

'Darcy, what are you doing here?' Scott put a hand on her shoulder, and she felt nauseated.

'I live here.' She didn't want to face him but looked up anyway and almost had to stop herself from laughing. He was now a blonde with a heavy, fake tan. She felt Trudy kick her from under the table and heard her snigger under her scarf.

'You do? Since when?' he asked.

Darcy couldn't believe she was shedding tears over the idiot not so long ago. 'Since August, not that it's any of your business now, eh?' She felt good for standing up to him.

'Darcy, I thought you'd be fine by now...'

'Can you believe this?' she said to Trudy and got up.

She felt Scott tug her coat as she was leaving. 'Please, Darce, let me explain...'

She squeezed past the queue and went outside, her chest heavy with emotion.

'Scott, just leave her alone,' said Trudy.

Scott stepped in front of her, grabbing her arms. 'I want to say how sorry I am...'

'Fine, you're sorry, can we now get on with our lives, please?' she begged, wanting to go and meet Gareth.

Scott bent forward and gave her a kiss on the cheek.

'I wish you hadn't done that.' Darcy took a deep breath. 'Fine. I've moved on now, so I guess we can be civil to each other. It was nice seeing you, Scott. Merry Christmas.'

She left him standing on the pavement as she turned away, grateful she had the chance to say her part.

'All end that ends well?' said Trudy, walking in step with her.

'I feel so much better now. Jeez, what possessed him to dye his hair though?' Darcy burst out laughing.

'Yeah, you've healed. Time to move on.'

'I have. Right, I'll leave you here because he'll be meeting me in another five minutes.'

'Alright, I'll catch you later.' She pulled her in for a hug.

Hugging her coffee cup for warmth, Darcy waited outside a busy department store, looking at the sea of faces as they passed. Twenty minutes went by, and there was still no sign of him. She got her mobile and called him, but the phone kept ringing. Her feet were ice cold, and after a further ten minutes of texting and calling, she decided to hop on the next bus back to the pub, downhearted and confused.

Chapter Thirteen

The following morning, Darcy strolled into the bar, half asleep with a blanket draped around her shoulders.

'What's with the long face?' asked her father, who was busy sweeping the floor.

'My date didn't show up yesterday.' She pulled out a chair and sat down. Darcy could talk to her father about anything.

'The guy from upstairs?'

'Yes, who do you think?'

'Oh, bloody hell.' He slapped his forehead and rested the sweeping brush against the bar. 'Darcy, did you get my message I left you on your phone?'

She sat up. 'No, what message?' She pulled her phone out of her dressing gown pocket. 'Why, what's happened?' She couldn't find any such message.

'Gareth popped in yesterday just as you left with Trudy. An emergency came up at home. He had to travel back to Dorset yesterday.'

'What? Here's me thinking he didn't want to know me anymore. But why didn't he call me?'

'I told him I'd pass on the message. He was in such a rush, Darcy. Don't blame him, blame me. This is all my fault.'

She flipped through her messages again and found a message from Gareth that hadn't long come through.

Hi,

Sorry about yesterday. I'm in Dorset at the moment. See the selfie. I'll call you as soon as possible and explain everything.'

Gx

'I feel like an idiot,' she exhaled and put her phone on the table.

'When are you ever going to learn not to jump to conclusions? I'll go and make us a coffee. Isn't it your barmaid's fashion show today?' he asked, making his way through the living area.

Darcy sniffed back tears. 'Yeah, it is. We've also got some YouTube star coming to film it, too.'

She took another look at his picture, smiled, and wrote him back.

I hope everything is ok? Missed you yesterday.

She had just got up from the chair when a reply came through.

Sorry, Darce. I'll make it up to you when I get back, promise. Having a bit of a family emergency, will text soon.

She went into her room and got changed into her 40's clothes and then went to open the pub. She stepped outside onto the pavement and crossed her arms for warmth. Traffic whizzed by, and people passed by, but there was no Mr. Jones.

Strange.

She went back inside the pub. 'Everything alright?' asked her dad.

Darcy shrugged. 'Yeah, I suppose,' she said and went to put some music on.

'Penny for your thoughts?' Jess intoned, with an entourage behind her. 'Did you find out where Gareth got to yesterday?' she asked.

'I did. He's back in Dorset. A family emergency or something.'

'See, I told you it was nothing to worry about. So, are you looking forward to today?' she asked while pointing instructions to her friends carrying all sorts of things for the show.

'You know I am. It's going to be fab,' she smiled and went to serve the group of students crowded at the bar.

'It looks like we've actually stepped back in time,' Darcy said looking around her hectic bar.

People of all ages were dressed in 1940s clothes. Men wore hats and suits and women in Land Army outfits and ARP uniforms.

Someone had got up on the stage, tapped the mic to get everyone's attention.

'Who's that man at the bar?' Darcy asked. 'He's been sitting there for over an hour nursing his pint.'

'No idea, never seen him in here before. Is he with the college?'

'No, never seen him before,' replied Jess.

Darcy went behind the bar. 'Can I get you anything else?' she asked the guy nursing his half- finished glass of beer.

'Are you Darcy Tanner?' he asked.

'I am. Do I know you?'

'No, but you know my father, Mr. Jones?'

'Yes,' she replied, panicking there was something wrong with him. 'Is there anything wrong?' She was surprised he had never mentioned his son to her.

'He's a bit under the weather at the moment. He asked me to come and tell you in case you wondered where he is.'

'Oh, I hope it's nothing too serious.'

'Just a chest infection.'

'I'm sorry, I wasn't aware he had a son.'

He laughed. 'He's very private. I understand you know who he is now?'

'Yes, I guess that makes us cousins, then?'

'That's right. It's such a relief that things are out in the open. I don't know why he has been a stubborn bugger over all this.'

'I don't think anyone was more shocked than I was.'

Chapter Fourteen

Darcy switched off the television, scoffing over the report that a cold snap called *The Beast From the East* was due to hit all of the UK by the end of the week.

'There'll be pandemonium at the supermarkets, you watch,' she remarked to her father sat on the sofa eating toast.

He nodded, still chewing. 'I still think you'd better get a food delivery done, just in case.'

Darcy laughed, putting on her coat. 'I believe it when I see it,'

She picked up her bag and the fresh cake she had made. 'I'm off to see Mr. Jones, see if he's alright. I can't believe it though, can you, Dad?'

Dylan swallowed his toast and took a gulp of his coffee. 'No, poor bugger. Why didn't he ever tell you, or even try to contact us? But,' he rose to feet, taking his empty dishes into the kitchen, 'at least he has a family now, that's all that matters.'

'Yeah, bless him. I hope he can make it to the wedding. Trudy said I could invite him,' she said, opening the living room door. 'See you later, and Dad, listen out for a call from the delivery people. It'll be about the order I made for the buffet.'

He didn't respond, but Darcy was sure he had heard and left the pub. She shivered as she stepped outside into the chilly air and made her way along Praed Street to the bus stop thinking how the weather report might be right for once.

Sitting in the bus shelter with the cake propped on her lap, she removed her glove with her teeth and then pulled her phone out of her pocket. She checked the note she had made of his address and searched for it on a map on her phone.

'What the hell!' she blurted out. 'How can this address not exist anymore?'

She researched his address and found that it was bombed during the war and that a new office development was built in its place.

Confused, she made her way back to the pub, hoping another regular may know where he lived.

'Sorry, Darcy. I haven't got a clue,' said Arthur playing a game of cards with his pal, Harry.

'Well, why did he give a fake address?'

The men both shrugged. 'He's very private, you know.' He looked at the cake tin in her hand. 'If there's any cake going spare...'

Darcy sighed heavily, thinking the best course of action was to wait until he came in for a drink. 'Sure, I'll get you both a piece.'

Chapter Fifteen

'Come on, we'd better get cleaning. Mam will be here soon,' Darcy collected the previous night's glasses and put them on the bar. There was no sign of Mr. Jones yet, which she thought was unusual.

'Aren't you going Christmas shopping with Trudy today?' asked her dad.

'Yeah, later on. Mam said she'd give you a hand behind the bar. And then tomorrow I've got to get this place spruced up for the wedding.'

'Calm down, love. Plenty of time,' he assured her with a pat on the arm.

'Easy for you to say,' she muttered. 'My friend is relying on me to give her a good wedding reception. Not to mention all the rich, business types that will be coming too.'

'Just be yourself, Darcy, and relax. I'll give you a hand, but first, go and meet your mother at the station, will you? No doubt she'll need help with her luggage. Did I tell you she bought a suitcase set from an auction site?'

'No, but she showed me the pictures. Leopard print, aren't they? So why can't you go?'

Dylan shrugged his shoulders.

'Not had an argument again, have you?'

'Only over her crazy Christmas spending, but what's new. It's probably why she bought the new suitcases to stuff all of her shopping in.'

Darcy opened the door, not in the least surprised to see the ground covered with snow. 'Looks like the weather report was right for once,' she hollered to her dad. 'There must be at least another two inches of snow here.'

'What's that?' he asked, joining her by the door. 'Bloody heck! See, I told you, didn't I? At least the station is only up the road.'

Darcy got on her warm, camel coloured 40's coat belonging to her great gran. 'See you in a minute,' she said as she left the bar. She walked along the snow-covered pavement, passed The Hilton, turned the corner and walked down to the station's entrance. A steady flow of disgruntled people was coming out of its entrance. That didn't bode too well, she thought. Once inside, Darcy stood on tiptoe, looking around at the sea of faces for her mother, while the voice over the tannoy was talking about possible cancellations due to the weather. She found the train that had just arrived from Swansea and waited with her arms folded to keep her warm.

'Come on,' she shivered as cold draught slashed the back of her legs. By the turnstiles, she saw a woman with dark hair wave at her.

'Mam, over here,' she sashayed around the crowd of people coming at her and went to meet her mother, dragging three suitcases behind her.

'Darcy, baby.' She put down her suitcases and pulled her in for a hug. 'Oh, I've missed you.'

'Missed you too, Mam,' Darcy smiled, catching a whiff of her mother's floral perfume.

Sandra stepped back, appraising Darcy's new look. 'You look stunning. Is this part of the plan for the pub?' she asked, passing her a suitcase and her handbag.

Darcy hooked the bag over her shoulder and took one of the suitcases. 'Yeah. Wow, what have you got in here?'

'Presents,' she beamed.

They began walking towards the station's entrance. 'Dad's not happy with the credit cards getting bashed again,' she laughed. 'He just had a moan before I left.'

'He moans every year but he's the first one to wake on Christmas morning like an excited child. So, do I get serve behind the bar? I've always fancied myself as a Bet Lynch from Coronation Street.'

'Mam, I think you're more like Kat Slater and that's going back a bit. I can't remember the last time I watched soaps,' Darcy laughed.

'SO THAT'S THE PUB TOUR,' Darcy said to her mother, who went to serve behind the bar like a natural.

Remembering the wedding food, Darcy looked for her father in a sea of faces across the pub floor. 'Dad?' she called, but he was busy sitting around the table with a group of older gentlemen. She huffed her way around the bar, excusing herself through a tight knit of people and tapped him on the shoulder.

'What's up?'

'The wedding food. Did you hear anything?'

'No, not a thing.'

'Oh no.' She pulled out her phone from her back pocket and checked her emails. She felt as though she'd been kicked in the stomach when she read that they were unable to deliver due to the snow.

'This is a nightmare. Mam,' she said. She thought she'd better check the cake shop, so she brought up their number and called them. There was no answer. It was then that she saw a text from Gareth.

Hey, there's no easy way to say this, Darce, but there's heavy snow here. I'm hoping to be back for Christmas. In fact, I'm going to do my absolute best to be back for Christmas. Don't worry. I hope the wedding preparations are going OK? We are losing the mobile signal now and then, so if you can't get a hold of me, try not to worry. Missing you.

'Oh, Mam, it's just one thing after another lately,' she cried. 'There's heavy snow in the West Country so he doesn't know if he can make it back.' Upset, she left the pub and went into her room. She closed the door behind her, not wanting to be disturbed, but she knew that would be impossible with a pub full of guests. There was a tap at her bedroom door.

'Is everything alright?' asked Jess, standing in the doorway.

'Not really,' Darcy sniffed back tears. 'The wedding is turning into a disaster. The food can't be delivered, and the cake shop isn't answering.'

'I can see that's going to be a problem. What are we going to feed the guests?'

Darcy shrugged. 'No idea, I have ruined my best friend's wedding and on top of that Gareth might not make it in time for Christmas.'

'Oh, Darce,' Jess came into the room, putting an arm around her. 'We're a team, remember? It'll all turn out for the best, you watch.'

'Yeah,' she pulled out her phone from her pocket. 'I hope so.' She texted him back.

I really wish you could be here. The wedding is turning into a catastrophe. The food can't be delivered and I'm at breaking point. Need a hug.

In a matter of seconds, a reply came through.

I'm doing my best, honest. Think about how they coped during the war when all they had were rations. Hint, hint! x

'I swear he's a bloody genius,' she said. 'If she wants an authentic 40's wedding, she's bloody well going to get one.'

'What's that?' asked Jess.

'A 1940s wedding wouldn't have had all the trappings of the 21st century, wouldn't it?'

Jess clocked on. 'Oh, you're right and it's a brilliant idea, but what will Trudy think of it?'

'Bugger Trudy. It's out of our hands now. I'll go to the supermarket, see what they got left and I guess we'll just have to wing it.'

'I'll come with you, but we better be quick. People are clearing the shelves.'

Darcy got her coat and left the pub with Jess. 'There's only Tesco up the road, we'll just have to see what we can find and use our imaginations.'

Walking up the snow-covered pavement, Darcy reached down, gathered a ball of snow and chucked it at Jess. 'Tag, you're it,' she laughed.

Chapter Sixteen

'I think this wedding is going to be a disaster,' cried Trudy on the phone.

Darcy had just finished icing the cake and looked up at the clock. It was 4.a.m. 'How? Everything is fine here.' She put the bowl in the sink thinking if only she knew what she had to go through to get everything sorted.

'At least fifteen people cancelled. saying the snow was making the journey impossible.'

Darcy thought about Gareth. 'Yeah, I know how you feel. Look, the people who matter to you the most will be here. Now, get some beauty sleep, will you?'

'Why are you up so early?'

'You rang,' she lied, determined she wouldn't tell her about the food delivery.

'But you sound quite awake. I didn't wake you up, did I?'

Rolling her eyes, Darcy headed for bed herself. 'No, now get some sleep. I'll see you in a few hours.'

Woken by her alarm at seven, Darcy sat up and heard her mother and father talking in the pub. 'Is everything alright, Mam?' she shouted but thought she'd better get dressed and sort out the pub for the wedding.

'Everything's fine, Darce,' said her mother when she finally walked into the bar. She looked around at all the decorations and flowers. 'Thanks for doing this,' she said, exhausted.

'No bother, love.' Her mother unfolded a white tablecloth and draped it over the table. 'No news about your boyfriend?'

'Nothing. I guess if he can't make it tonight, then there's nothing I can do about it.' She tried to remain rational about the situation and promptly got off the stool to take a shower and get ready for the service.

By ten o'clock, Darcy was ready and in full make-up for the first arrivals at eleven. While she helped her mother in the kitchen prepping the salad, Jess called her into the pub.

'You got a visitor,' she yelled.

Darcy popped her head around the door, surprised to see Mr. Jones accompanied by another, much younger man.

'Mr. Jones, I'm so glad you could make it.'

'Enough of the Mr. Jones, call me Sam,' he said. 'I'd like to formally introduce you to my son, James. James, this is Darcy.'

'Your son? Haven't we met before?' she said, shaking his hand.

'I came to tell you about Dad. Sorry, I didn't introduce myself properly, you know how stubborn he has been about telling the family who he was.'

'I know too well. So, what will it be, a pint?' she asked when her dad emerged from the bathroom with a mop bucket in hand. 'Dad, I'd like you to meet James, Sam's son.'

'Gosh this pub has turned up some history, hasn't it,' he stuck out his hand. 'It's almost like an episode of Time Team,' he chuckled. 'So, this makes us cousins, right?'

'It does. Nice to meet you.'

'You too. I'm sorry we didn't get to know each other sooner.'

'Things happen for a reason, I guess. We should meet up for a proper reunion one day.'

'Why don't you both come for Christmas dinner?' asked Darcy. 'There's plenty of room.'

'That would be fantastic,' James replied. 'I think Dad would love that.'

'So that's sorted then,' said Dylan.

'So, I hate to break up this family reunion, but I have a wedding to sort out, now excuse me gents.' As she went back into her living quarters, her phone rang.

'Merry Christmas,' said Gareth. 'How are you?'

'I'm okay, you know, busy with this wedding. So, are you going to make it?'

'I'm trying, I promise. If I don't, then I want you to have a nice Christmas, alright. Don't let my absence spoil it for you.'

'I'll try, but it's going to be difficult because I miss you.'

'I miss you too. Very much.'

There was a clatter of glass smashing. Darcy jumped. 'I'd better go and see what's happened.'

'I'll call you later.'

Darcy rushed into the kitchen, horrified to find that her mother had dropped a tray of wine glasses. 'Oh, Mam,' she cried, on the verge of tears.

'Don't stress, just go and wait for the guests. I'll clean this up.'

Darcy took a slow exhale, leaving her mother to clean up the mess. 'You wouldn't think it's Christmas with all this going on, would you?' she said to Mr. Jones as she went to open the pub. Aside from the blast of cold air that surprised her, a woman was standing by the door, ready to knock. She was holding the biggest bunch of red roses Darcy had ever seen.

'Miss Tanner?' she asked, reading the card. She looked up at Darcy and then handed her the flowers. 'These are for you.'

'Me?' Darcy exclaimed. 'Thank you.'

'You're welcome. I was just about to shut shop for the day,' the woman said. 'I doubt we'd get many customers in this weather.'

'I know, the snow is coming down heavier, isn't it?' Darcy read the card.

If I don't make it back, have a lovely Christmas. Love you.

'He was lucky he caught me in the shop so early.'

'Who?' she asked, now noticing there was no name on the card. Thinking it had to be Gareth, she thanked the lady and read the note again. 'Gosh, he loves me,' she whispered and then realised she had said it out loud.

'I love a bit of mystery. Hope he makes it home, Merry Christmas.'

'Thanks, and yes, Merry Christmas to you.'

'Who was that?' asked her mother, looking over her shoulder. 'Oh, they're beautiful, are they for the wedding?'

'No,' she replied, stepping inside the pub. 'They're from Gareth.'

She went to the kitchen and put them in a vase. A smile stretched across her face that was hard not to notice.

'So, he's coming back tonight?' asked Jess.

'It doesn't seem like it.'

She grabbed her mobile from the counter and text him to say thank you for the flowers.

'Oh well, I'm sure he'll let me know if he can make it or not, now what do you want me to do?' she asked, with a new-found spring to her step, despite feeling cold.

Her mother handed her a tray of sandwiches which she took into the pub.

'There's a problem,' cried Trudy on the phone. 'The bloody registrar can't get in.'

Darcy took a deep breath, cussed, and then covered the speaker on her phone. 'Woah, wait up everyone. The registrar can't get in.' She raised a hand for them to hush and then went back on the phone. 'What are you going to do?'

'I don't know. My whole day is ruined because of that bloody white stuff.'

Darcy didn't know what to do and looked around the room for suggestions.

'There's a church up the road. I'll go and ask the vicar if he's willing to help out,' said Mr. Jones.

Darcy gave him a thumbs up. 'We may be able to get a vicar, so get ready. I'll see you in a bit.' She exhaled and switched off her phone. Her father said he'd go with Mr. Jones and left the pub.

'What a start to the day, eh?' She poured herself a glass of wine and looked up at the clock. It wasn't even midday.

'At least the wedding can still go ahead,' said her mother. 'Not sure how Harvey will feel about exchanging vows in a pub, but serves him right for picking the busiest night of the year.'

Darcy laughed, spitting out a bit of her wine. 'Looks like the first lot of guests are arriving.' She gave a nod to the window where a minivan had parked on the roadside. 'I think I'd better go and welcome them. I won't be a minute.'

Darcy stood on the doorstep, shivering as she watched Trudy step out of the car looking elegant in her silk dress.

'It's not the way I'd hoped things would go, but how many can say they had a white wedding?' She flashed a genuine smile that put Darcy at ease.

'Come inside you must be freezing,' she said and then welcomed her parents to the pub.

'Darce, I'll just go and wait in the back until Harvey comes,' said Trudy.

'Yes, I'll be with you in a moment.' Flustered, she greeted another lot of Trudy's family into the pub and then went to check on her in the back room.

'Everything alright?' she asked, walking into the room where Trudy's bridesmaids were fussing over her.

'Did you arrange for the vicar to come?'

'Yes, don't panic,' she replied thinking how her father hadn't come back yet. 'You look gorgeous, let me take a photo of everyone.' She picked her mobile up from the coffee table and as she was about to assemble everyone, she heard the floorboards creak above her. She looked up.

'What's the matter?' asked Trudy also looking up at the ceiling.

'Did you hear the floorboards creak?'

'No.'

'Weird.'

'Isn't whatshisname back yet?'

'You mean Gareth. No, he isn't,' she said, gloomily.

The living room door burst open, bringing with it the noise of the now packed pub. 'Darce, the vicar will be here in half-hour,' said her father. 'I said you'd bung him a few pints, alright?'

'Yeah of course.'

'And Harvey has arrived, so I'll keep him out of trouble for a bit,' he winked and then left the room.

Darcy turned to Trudy. 'There, no panic now. I still can't believe we pulled it off.'

Trudy raised her eyes to the ceiling.

'What?' asked Darcy, following her gaze.

'I think you're right; I think there may be someone up there.'

'Well I can't let myself in to look,' said Darcy. 'It's not right.'

'Phone to see if he's home.'

Darcy rang his number, but it went straight to the answer machine.

'Hey, it's me. Are you home yet because I thought I heard you upstairs? Anyway, miss you. Talk soon.'

'You're his girlfriend and landlord for God's sake, if you think there's something wrong you have every right to check it out. Go, quickly...'

While everyone was busy, Darcy went into the hallway and turned the handle of the door leading upstairs to Gareth's flat. She stood at the bottom, waiting for a reply or an indication that he was home, but there was nothing.

'Strange.'

'Everything alright?' her mother asked.

Everyone had now taken their seats which had been arranged into rows.

'Have you seen the vicar?' asked.

Thinking he hadn't shown up, she covered her mouth with her hand. 'Don't tell me he can't make it now?'

'No,' she whispered. 'You've got to see what he's turned up in.' She laughed and covered her face.

Darcy looked around the room, catching Harvey's horrified expression.

'What's happened?' As she spoke, she caught something red appearing from the bathroom at the corner of her eye. 'Is that...?'

'That's the vicar, alright.'

The vicar gave her a wave wearing a Father Christmas suit.

She slowly raised her hand to her mouth, forcing herself not to laugh. 'Trudy is going to go mental,' she whispered.

'She's going to have to put up with it. Besides, he's dressed for the occasion, isn't he?'

'Oh, Mam, don't make a joke of it will you? Do I tell Trudy or give her a surprise when she comes out?' she asked and thought it was best to let her know.

When she went back into the living area, Trudy was standing by the door to the upstairs flat. 'What's the matter?' asked Darcy.

'I think you were right; someone must be up there.'

'I'll look in a moment but first, you are going to want to hear this.'

'Oh no, what's gone wrong now?'

'It's the vicar. He's wearing a Santa suit.' She laughed, not meaning to.

'You're kidding?' She went to take a look, but Darcy stopped her.

'He was helping out at a local hospital, so count yourself lucky he could step in at the last minute.'

'Can this day get any more bizarre?'

'There are still at least twelve hours to go, so who knows.'

Darcy stood at the bottom of the stairs, bit her lip, and thought she 'd take a look. Tentatively, she walked up the stairs, and got to the top of the landing and tapped lightly on the door. She felt like an idiot as she knew there was nobody home.

Shuffling could be heard inside, and Darcy stepped back.

'Hi, is there anyone home?' she asked and twisted the door handle. To her surprise, the door swung open. At first, she thought Gareth had come home, but when she stepped into the living room, the place was empty.

The curtain blew, and Darcy jumped and walked straight into the coffee table. 'Oh my God,' she screamed, and then realised the window had been left open ajar. She pushed herself up from the table and happened to notice a black and white photograph. She picked it up and covered her mouth with her hand. It was a picture of her grandmother with a man she thought at first was Gareth.

'All ok?' asked Trudy.

Darcy handed her the picture, unable to speak.

'Is this your guy?' she asked, stunned by the likeness.

'No, it's definitely the 40's, and that's definitely my grandmother.'

'So. what's it doing here?'

'I don't know. I found it on the table.' Darcy walked up and down the room, checking the kitchen and the bedroom. 'I did hear someone in here, I swear I did.'

'I don't know what to say, Darce. But you want to check out this guy. What was his name again?'

'I can't remember, I'll go and ask Mr. Jones, see if he can shed some light on this.'

Darcy ran back downstairs, into the hubbub of the pub.

'Alright, Darce?' asked her father as she stood in the doorway looking for Mr. Jones.

'Huh?' she turned to face him. 'Sorry, Dad, I can't talk a minute...' She saw Mr. Jones leaving the pub and sashayed around the customers to the exit. The snow was chucking it down, and she stood on the pavement, yelling after him.

'Where are you going?' she said, eventually catching up with him.

'Did you find the picture?' he asked.

'That was you?'

'My job here is done, Darcy. It's time for me to go home.'

Darcy shook her head quizzically. 'What on earth do you mean? You live that way, don't you?' She pointed towards the pub.

His voice softened. 'Darcy, it was never a coincidence that your grandmother left you the pub. It was always meant to be yours.'

'Sorry, I don't quite follow.' She held out the photograph. 'Mr. Jones, Walter looks like Gareth. How?'

'You see, Darcy, sometimes, the past will play out throughout multiple lifetimes until there's a happier ending to the story. It's nothing to be concerned about.'

Darcy shook her head. 'This is bizarre, Mr. Jones... I ... Who are you? I mean, really?'

Mr. Jones smiled and put a hand on her shoulder. 'I'm your friend.'

'So where are you going? Will we ever see you again?' she shouted to him walking down the street.

'I'll be popping in from time to time, don't you worry...' He waved. 'Oh, and I haven't forgotten about your offer of Christmas dinner.'

'Darcy?' shouted her dad.

She turned around for a second and then looked back, but Mr. Jones had gone.

Dumbfounded, she walked into the pub.

'Why did you take off like that?' Her father asked.

'I... sorry, Dad, I can't talk a minute.'

'Well good, so I can finally say my bit. Gareth asked to meet you at Piccadilly Circus at 9 p.m.'

'What did you say?'

'I said...'

'No, I know what you said, but my ears can't believe it...' She edged her way through a small crowd of people standing outside the pub's entrance and went straight to her room.

'Is everything alright?' asked her mother, who opened the door.

Darcy began fixing her hair in the mirror, still shaken and reeling from everything that had happened today.

'I'm okay, Mam. I'll be out soon.'

'Dad said that Gareth asked to meet you tonight, is that right?'

'Yeah. Oh, Mam, remember when I told you about nana Lily and Walter?'

'Yeah, it's a lovely story. I've been telling all the women at work...'

'Well, tonight, on Christmas Eve, is when they should've met and ended up spending the rest of their lives together... isn't it an amazing coincidence that I'm meeting the love of my life tonight?'

Her mother smiled. 'It is the most magical time of the year, right? Anything is possible on Christmas Eve.'

Chapter Seventeen

Are you sure this is far enough?' Harvey asked, pulling his car up alongside the curb.

Darcy looked out the window at the deserted street. The snow was falling heavily.

'Yes, thank you both.' She opened the car door and was about to step outside. 'Hope you have a lovely Christmas and congratulations.'

'Thanks, Darce,' said Trudy from the back seat. 'I hope you find what you're looking for tonight. I'm so excited for you.'

'I'll tell you all about it in the morning.' She couldn't wipe the smile off her face.

'You'd better.'

Darcy waved them off and began walking up the snow-covered pavement. The sky was clear with stars, and the cold felt fresh on her face. The billboard lights at the corner of Piccadilly came into view, and Darcy stopped for a moment to let the moment sink in.

She took a deep breath, thinking of her nana and Walter when her phone pinged with a message.

'Oh,' she pulled her phone from her pocket.

Almost there.

Darcy headed to the stand, cupping her hands over mouth, blowing them for warmth. The area was quietest she had ever seen in London. Even the snow was fresh and untrodden upon.

She paced around the monument to keep warm while looking for Gareth, but the streets were a blur with snow falling heavily. Just then she heard footsteps crunching on snow, and turned around. A tall, dark figure appeared, walking toward her.

'Darcy?'

'Yes, it's me,' she cried, running into his open arms. 'It's so good to see you again.'

He held her tightly against his body. 'I missed you.' He pulled back and cupped his gloved hands on her face. 'I love you, Darcy. There's no doubt about that.' He paused for a moment, looking up at the billboard.

'What are you looking at?' she asked and then followed his gaze.

On the billboard, it said:

Merry Christmas, Darcy, and Gareth.

Darcy blinked. 'Did that say...' but when she focused in on the words they disappeared.

'I think so... it did say our names, right? I'm not imagining things, am I?' he asked, taking her hand.

'I saw it myself. It said Merry Christmas, Darcy, and Gareth.' Darcy laughed. 'That was sort of crazy, yeah?'

Gareth was still staring at the billboard and Darcy wondered if there was anything wrong.

'What is it?'

'I didn't tell you the reason I had to rush back home, did I?' He turned to face her.

'No,' she replied, shivering in the cold. Gareth pulled her in close.

'I found something out about our Walter.' His eyes settled on hers. 'He was my great grandfather.'

Darcy loosened her grip on his coat and stepped back. 'Are you kidding me?'

He shook his head, smiling. 'No. I can prove it to you with the documents my friend found. I didn't want to say anything to you in case it wasn't true.'

'So, my great nana and your great grandfather... but he didn't have children, did he?'

'Yes, he had a son out of wedlock before he left for the navy. I'm not even sure if he knew of his existence, if I'm honest. But Darcy... isn't it amazing how we found each other? And how our stories intertwine?'

'It's like we were meant to find each other... or... and this might sound even crazier than seeing our names on the billboard,' she paused, 'but what if we had a little helping hand from, you know, spirit or something?'

'Or Father Christmas's elves?' he laughed.

'Or maybe even that.' She found it amusing and threw her arms around him. 'But whatever it was,' she whispered as she rested her head on his shoulder. 'It's almost as if the story about my nan and Walter needed a happier ending.'